After All,
You're
Callie Boone

After All, You're Callie Boone

WINNIE MACK

Feiwel and Friends
New York

A FEIWEL AND FRIENDS BOOK
An Imprint of Macmillan

AFTER ALL, YOU'RE CALLIE BOONE. Copyright © 2010 by Winnie C. Smith.
All rights reserved. Distributed in Canada by H.B. Fenn and Company, Ltd.
Printed in May 2010 in the United States of America by
R. R. Donnelley & Sons Company, Harrisonburg, Virginia. For information, address
Feiwel and Friends, 175 Fifth Avenue, New York, N.Y. 10010.

Library of Congress Cataloging-in-Publication Data available

ISBN: 978-0-312-56331-8

Book design by Elizabeth Tardiff

Feiwel and Friends logo designed by Filomena Tuosto

First Edition: 2010

10 9 8 7 6 5 4 3 2 1

www.feiwelandfriends.com

For the Flower Girls: Karlee, Lindsey, Maya,
Naleigha, Peighton, and Zoe

And for my husband, Mike,
my very own Hoot

Chapter One

We were officially the weirdest family on the block.

The thing was, life had already been bad enough for me before that crummy afternoon when Uncle Danny parked his rusty Ford Escort in the driveway and started unloading pet carriers filled with furry brown ferrets into our garage.

But that didn't stop our two wiener dogs (Babs and Roger) from going ballistic, barking and leaping as high in the air as their stubby legs could carry them (like they'd actually know what to do with the ferrets if they caught them). And it didn't stop Grandma from rushing outside in her pink *nightgown*, practically foaming at the mouth because all the commotion was ruining *Oprah*.

When she saw the ferrets, Grandma let out a high-pitched scream that sounded almost exactly like the teakettle she boiled every afternoon. Then she started raving about a rat infestation.

And she kept going, even when Uncle Danny told her over and over again that they weren't rats at all (which they weren't. In fact, aside from their creepy hunched backs, they were surprisingly cute, which I realize is kind of beside the point), but Grandma was too busy freaking out to listen.

Dad pulled into the driveway, his Honda still making the funny banging noise that not even his mechanic could figure out. He looked confused as he climbed out of the car and adjusted his belt. (His belly was bigger than I'd ever seen it and even though I liked the solid roundness of it, Mom said it "had to go." For weeks she'd been trying to make him do morning calisthenics and pour flax-seed on his cereal.) His dark hair was neatly combed, the way it had to be at the bank, and his eyebrows were squished close together with concern.

He squinted through his new glasses to get a better look at the situation, and that was when he spotted the ferrets. His face, which was usually a completely normal color, turned the most amazing cartoon red. I half-expected steam to shoot out of his nostrils and I was sure that if anyone so much as tugged on his earlobe, his whole head would have exploded.

This all came as a shock because Dad was usually the calmest person within a twenty-mile radius.

Actually, make that forty miles.

Mom called him "the voice of reason."

I watched him take a deep breath, so deep he could have spent the next two weeks underwater.

And in the water was exactly where *I* would have rather been right then (and all the time, as a matter of fact).

The pool was the only place where I felt like nothing else mattered, and as I glanced away from my crazy front yard to the Elliots' house, knowing there was a beautiful crystal blue one (with a slide and a diving board!) behind the fence that no one even used, it almost drove me bonkers.

Some people didn't even know how lucky they were.

But I knew exactly how *unlucky* I was.

I sighed and turned my attention back to Dad, who was about to speak. When he did, he sounded like he was choking.

He asked Uncle Danny why on earth he'd brought the ferrets to our house when Danny himself was barely welcome in the spare bedroom. After all, Dad reminded him, he owed my parents over two thousand dollars in rent and they were starting to wonder if he was ever going to pay it back.

Uncle Danny didn't have a chance to say a word in his defense before Dad threw in a bit of guilt by reminding him that the money was supposed to go toward braces for my older brother, Kenneth. Even though Dad didn't say it out loud, we all knew what that meant: Kenneth would spend the tenth grade as bucktoothed (and weird-looking) as he'd been in the ninth.

Maybe even worse.

Under normal circumstances, this would have been bad enough, but Kenneth went to Edgevale High School, home of the Edgevale Beavers.

You do the math.

Then my mom raced around the corner in our minivan, the tires squealing like the freaking Indy 500, with a police car chasing her. Its lights were flashing and the siren howled loudly enough for Mr. Owens next door to run outside, where I could tell he was doing his best not to look at Grandma in her nightie. (What I couldn't tell was whether it was because, like me, he was scared of the bulging dark blue veins that ran down the backs of her legs or if he had some kind of old-people crush on her. The truth was, I probably didn't want to know.)

Anyway, Mom got out of the van and started explaining herself to us and the policeman, jabbing her car keys in the air with every third word, like she was stabbing mosquitoes. It turned out that she'd rolled through a stop sign, then refused to pull over for the policeman when he turned on his lights. She thought she had a good reason, though: My baby brother, Clayton, was going to wet his pants and she'd needed to get him home.

Fast.

Clay unbuckled his car seat himself, jumped out of the van, and ran across the lawn, tugging at his zipper. As she watched him, Mom sighed and told the policeman to go ahead and write the ticket. She raised her hands in surrender and admitted she was guilty, but wanted to make sure he understood that she couldn't let almost six months' worth of potty training go down the toilet.

Then Kenneth, who always has to be what Grandma calls a "smart aleck," reminded Mom that the toilet was exactly where she wanted it to go.

Mom grounded him on the spot.

This meant that, along with being stuck with his buckteeth for no one knew how much longer, he also wouldn't be able to go to some stupid concert he'd already bought tickets for.

My big brother, who looked like a ghost after spending most of his time locked in his bedroom listening to music and daydreaming about being a rock star, threw the kind of temper tantrum fifteen-year-olds don't usually throw in public because they're too busy trying to look cool, even when they're not.

And Kenneth was *not* cool.

Not even when he stood in front of the open refrigerator.

The policeman's mouth hung open, and I was pretty sure he was wishing he could turn around and walk away from the whole scene, just like I wished at that moment (and many others in the past eleven years, but that's also beside the point).

Instead of backing away slowly and trying to convince himself that my family was a figment of his imagination, the policeman pulled out his pad and started writing the ticket.

So, between the flashing lights of the squad car, the ferrets, the frantic wiener dogs, my hysterical grandmother, the toilet training, and Kenneth's spontaneous meltdown, the neighbors didn't have to take a vote, or even talk it over.

Everyone on the street just kind of *knew* that the Boone family was the weirdest.

Aside from the obvious but temporary embarrassment, all of this would have been okay, it really would have, but at that exact moment, when everyone seemed to be going crazy at once, I saw them, and the whole situation suddenly felt about ten times worse.

My very best friend since the first grade, Amy Higgins, was walking past the front of my house with her new best friend, Samantha McAllister.

I froze in my flip-flops.

Oh, fish sticks.

My mouth dried up and everything slowed down, like an instant replay on *Monday Night Football*.

While I watched from fifty feet away (which felt like a thousand miles), Amy pulled her blond ponytail over her shoulder and played with the ends while Samantha leaned in and whispered something that made Amy's eyes bug out. Then they both laughed, the way they had at the zoo when I ran into them at the penguin exhibit, and again at Sweet Dreams when my family went for ice cream on Grandma's birthday. I'd sat there, licking my stupid pistachio cone and gritting my teeth while Mom, who had no idea that we weren't friends anymore, smiled and waved to Amy from across the restaurant as though nothing was wrong.

But *everything* was wrong.

Seeing both of them laughing at the free circus in my front yard, I felt hollow inside, like there was nothing but stale air where my bones and organs were supposed to be.

Back when Amy was my best friend, she would have stood next to me and made me feel better. She would have told me that while her family might not be as crazy as mine, they were a very close second.

Why did she stop liking me and pick snotty Samantha McAllister to be her best friend instead?

Maybe it was because I didn't drool over Kevin Lee or Steven Benson, like Samantha did.

Or maybe it was because I liked riding my bike more than painting my fingernails.

The thing was, Amy used to love riding bikes, too. In fact, she used to like *all* the same stuff as me, until she suddenly changed and decided none of it was "awesome" anymore.

And that meant *I* wasn't awesome anymore either.

It started just before the school year ended, when Amy didn't meet me at our usual recess spot to trade stickers with the other kids. I joined in anyway, but kept checking the door to see if she was on her way out and worrying that she was sick, in trouble with Ms. Midland, or something even worse.

When I asked her about it later, she said she didn't feel like "messing around with stickers" so she'd stayed inside instead.

The next day, I couldn't find her at lunch, and it turned out that even though it was hot dog day in the cafeteria (our favorite), she'd gone home with Samantha to eat veggie burgers and work on an assignment for social studies together.

I had the same assignment, but they hadn't invited me along.

The idea made my stomach twist.

Even though I knew something wasn't quite right between us, I tried to act like it was.

Then Amy started telling me she was "busy" in the afternoons and "had plans" on the weekends when normally we would have had a sleepover (on at least one of the nights).

Nosy Beth Oberman was the one who clued me in after almost a whole month of not knowing what was going on or what to do about it. She flat out told me that Amy didn't want to hang out with me anymore, and the superior look on her face when she lied like that was enough to make me hate her.

I told her to buzz off, figuring she was either crazy or jealous, and headed for my locker.

That's when I overheard Amy and Samantha talking.

About me.

"Callie's so stupid, she doesn't even *get it*," Samantha said.

My ears filled with a rushing sound as I leaned against the wall. I was as quiet and still as I could be.

What didn't I get?

My palms were sweating and I held my breath.

"I know," Amy said. Then, instead of telling Samantha that we were best friends, she added, "Even though we're the same age, it's like she's a baby sister who keeps trying to tag along."

Tag along?

My cheeks were burning hot and tears prickled my eyes.

"I don't know how you could stand her for so long."

"Me neither," Amy said. "She's a *loser*."

I turned away before I heard anything else and ran for the door.

I shoved it open just as my hands started to shake.

Why?

The word flashed like a neon sign over and over again in my head.

I took a big gulp of fresh air as the door squeaked shut behind me. I leaned against it, as if I could keep what I'd overheard from following me home.

But I knew I couldn't.

I couldn't believe what Amy had said, and my head spun, trying to come up with a reason for it.

Why?

As I wiped my sweaty hands on my shorts, all I wanted was to be at home, curled up in a ball on my bed.

Instead, I checked out the scene in front of me.

The school yard was packed with kids in groups of two, three, and more. Some were huddled together to talk, or passing a basketball, and others were waving good-bye to their friends as their moms picked them up.

Aside from me, the only person who stood alone was the crossing guard, waiting for the next batch of kids.

Well, him and a first grader with his finger up his nose.

I took another deep breath and almost choked on it.

My very best friend on the planet had called me a loser.

A *loser.*

Big fat tears filled both of my eyes, and I blinked hard a few times to stop them from overflowing.

Nosy Beth Oberman hadn't lied.

Amy really didn't want to be best friends anymore.

Why?

What did I do wrong?

I couldn't think of a single thing that would make her stop liking me.

We told jokes, played games, watched TV, sang along with the car radio, braided each other's hair, traded books, and shared secrets.

We did everything together.

For as long as I could remember.

My throat was so dry and tight, it hurt to swallow.

She wanted to be friends with *Samantha McAllister* instead? Samantha McAllister, who was supposed to be best friends with Julie Foster?

She had her own stupid best friend!

And Amy had me!

Why was this happening?

And how could I fix it?

Another pair of tears made everything blurry and this time I wiped them away with the backs of my hands.

"Callie, are you okay?" Mrs. Banner asked, walking toward me with a worried look.

I had to think fast.

"Yes," I told her, moving away from the building and down the stairs. "I have allergies."

"Maybe the school nurse—"

"It's okay," I said, hating the quiver in my voice. "I have stuff at the house."

"Very well, then," she said as I walked past her. "Enjoy your summer."

"I will," I lied.

How was I supposed to enjoy a summer without Amy?

How was I supposed to enjoy *anything*?

I wondered if Amy and Samantha were still talking about me, right that second, and I wanted to run back inside the school and tell them to stop.

But even more, I wanted to run away from the school, from Amy, from all the kids who didn't look like they had anything to worry about but whether they'd make the next basket.

So I left.

On the lonely walk home, I used every bit of strength I had to not let a single tear fall, which was almost impossible.

If I hadn't been too embarrassed to tell Mom (or anyone else) what had happened, she would have patted me on the back and congratulated me on "sucking it up."

But if sucking it up meant barely managing to stop myself from bursting into tears and begging Amy to tell me why she dumped me, then sucking it up . . . *sucked.*

It had barely started, but it had already been the longest summer of my life. For the first time ever, I wasn't looking forward to going back to school in September. Instead of planning a trip to the mall with Amy, where we'd shop for supplies from the sixth-grade list together, I hung out at home and dreaded that first day back, when I'd have to walk up the front steps of Lincoln Middle School, with no best friend next to me and no idea who I'd eat lunch with.

Sometimes I'd forget about Amy for a little while, if I was busy with something else, like giving Clayton a bath or reading a good book, but then I'd suddenly remember again and a horrible feeling came over me, like I might throw up.

I wasn't scared, exactly, but worried, because I wasn't sure how much had changed. I wasn't sure whether not being best friends meant not being friends *at all.*

I didn't know if I'd be invited to her birthday parties and sleepovers, or if I'd ever be welcome in Amy's house again *and I hadn't even done anything wrong*!

I missed her mom's chocolate chip walnut cookies and the way we all teased Mr. Higgins about his goofy bed-head when he made French toast for us kids on Sunday mornings.

I'd missed having a best friend from the very second school ended, but the moment I missed her the most was that afternoon with the ferrets, when she was only a few steps away from my house.

While I watched Amy and Samantha make fun of my family from across the street, I reached for the red-and-blue braided friendship bracelet my *ex*-best friend had made for me. It was double-knotted around my wrist.

Was she still wearing the one I made for her?

When we'd exchanged them, we'd both solemnly promised to wear them forever.

Just thinking about it made me want to cry.

I wished I could just waltz over there and start a conversation, as though nothing had ever happened between us.

But I couldn't.

I wished my whole family was inside the house, acting like normal human beings.

But they weren't.

Instead they were acting like lunatics and showing Amy that she was probably right about me.

Maybe I *wasn't* cool enough to be her best friend.

I sighed as Amy and Samantha turned to walk toward Jefferson Park, whispering and snickering more with every step.

I watched Mom accept her ticket, the rest of the family walk back into the house, and the police car slowly drive away.

And while I stood in the shadows of the garage, like a big, lonely lump of loser, I tried to pretend none of it mattered.

But of course it did.

Chapter Two

Callie, you're missing the whole summer," Mom said, tugging at my blankets. She marched over to my window and opened my blinds, so bright sunshine streamed directly into my face.

Nice.

"Mom, can you please close the—"

"Hey, vacations only last so long, and you'll be kicking yourself when this one's over."

"Urgh," I groaned, pulling the sheet over my head.

Of course, thin cotton wasn't enough to block out her voice.

"Mrs. Crisp's going to be here in ten minutes to take you to the pool. I need you dressed and ready, with your bed made, in eight minutes."

"Why do I have to make the bed?" I grumbled. "I'm only going to mess it up again tonight."

"Nice try, honey. Seven and a half minutes and counting. Let's move."

"I'm moving," I sighed.

Rolling out of bed, I wished (for at least the eight millionth time) that Mom had never been a drill sergeant. I was pretty sure her college students wished for the exact same thing.

I slipped into my purple bathing suit, covered it up with capris and a red T-shirt, grabbed my flip-flops, tossed my sunscreen, baseball hat, and a towel into my backpack, and started toward the door.

The community pool.

And just like that, all of my tiredness slipped away as I imagined the crystal blue water I'd be diving into.

"Don't forget about the bed," Mom shouted from the kitchen.

Unbelievable! It was like she had X-ray vision or something.

I pulled my sheets and flowered bedspread back into place and tossed my pillows on top, before turning to leave.

Catching my reflection in the mirror on the back of my bedroom door, I saw my bobbed dark brown hair—still a little wild from sleep—the blue eyes that matched my dad's, and the upturned nose I absolutely hated. At least I had a bit of a tan, or a "healthy glow," as Mom liked to call it.

As practice for September, I smiled and told the mirror I'd had an awesome summer, but it was obvious from the weird tone of my voice that the lie still needed work.

Sighing, I left the comfortable silence of my bedroom and stepped into the hall, where Clayton, wearing only pull-ups and a Superman cape, shouted something that sounded like "Yar!" and whacked my shins with a cardboard tube.

"Good morning," I said, resting my hand on the top of his dark, curly head. It was partly out of love but mostly to hold him back.

He whacked me again.

"Quit it, Clay."

And again.

"Clay, I'm serious!"

"Thee-wee-uth," he screeched, this time aiming for my head.

"Mom!" I called, hoping for backup.

"Clayton," she warned from the kitchen.

Even at three years old, Clay knew her tone meant big trouble and he stopped to think about it for a second before he gave me an evil grin, then came at me with another "Yar!"

He hit my shoulder, and this time I screamed louder than truly necessary.

Maybe I should sign up for drama next year.

Never mind.

Amy loved that class, so she'd probably sign up with Samantha.

Mom appeared at the bottom of the stairs with her hands on her hips, wearing a scowl that meant business. Her hair was pulled back in a tight bun, and I doubted a single strand would be brave enough to attempt an escape.

"Clayton Morris Boone," she said sternly. "Drop your weapon and get to the table."

I was amazed the Marine Corps had let her retire.

Clayton wailed, in a combination of embarrassment and frustration, then plopped onto the top step to pout.

"You'd better get to the table, buddy," I whispered, knowing from experience that Mom was pretty cranky on Thursdays, when she had a full schedule to teach.

"Clay," Mom warned, her voice dropping to a level I knew was dangerous, "if I have to count to three, your name will be Mud."

I smiled to myself. The Clay-to-Mud line was a family joke, but my brother was too little to get it. The truth was, he was too little to get much beyond Froot Loops and fart jokes.

I reached for his hand, which was sticky, as usual (from what, I didn't even want to imagine), and walked him down the stairs, where Mom thanked me for helping out and gave my shoulders a squeeze.

I always liked it when she did that. We were the only girls in the house (unless you counted Grandma, and I didn't, really. I'm pretty sure she'd never been a girl) but we weren't close like Dad and me.

Mom always seemed too busy to goof around.

I looked at the table, where Kenneth was hunched over his *Spin* magazine, making gross slurping noises as he shoveled soggy Rice Krispies into his mouth. Grandma blew on her cup of peppermint tea, then winced when she burned her tongue anyway, and Uncle Danny hummed to himself as he read the sports section of the newspaper.

I saw Dad lick his lips as he reached for the plate of bacon.

"Bill," Mom warned.

He was supposed to be watching his cholesterol.

And he was watching it . . . *go up.*

"Just one more piece," he said, smiling and poking the pile with his fork to find the biggest, crispiest slice.

"Well, that's another set of push-ups you owe me." Mom frowned.

"Which bumps your IOU up to about six thousand," Kenneth joked, but neither Mom nor Dad was laughing.

Poor Dad. He couldn't help the fact that he loved cookie dough ice cream, mashed potatoes, *and* bacon. (Not all together, of course, although I wouldn't put it past him.)

I gave him a sympathetic smile as I joined the rest of my family at the table.

The plate of bacon was passed to me, followed by a bowl of scrambled eggs. I preferred mine over easy, but knew not to say anything. If I did, Mom would give her usual speech, which always ended with either "until you start cooking, I don't want to hear about it" or "there's yogurt in the fridge."

"Off to the pool today?" Dad asked.

"Yup," I said, starting to smile.

"I'm jealous. A nice swim sure beats the meetings I've got scheduled." He took a sip of coffee. "You think you can squeeze in a few laps?"

Oh, fish sticks.

"Dad, the outdoor pool doesn't even have lanes," I reminded him.

"So?" Grandma asked.

"So it's not like the aquatic center. It's packed with kids and it's mostly playing and splashing."

"Ahh," Grandma said, nodding. "You still don't like the laps."

I didn't want her to know she was right. "No, I just—"

"If you want to be good, you've got to do the work," Dad reminded me.

I *knew* that. How could I *not* know that? "I will, when you and I practice."

"Good kid," Dad said with a smile.

"I see the new people are moving into the Lius' house," Mom said, looking next door as she rinsed the soap from a frying pan.

"Really?" I asked, excited at the thought. The "sold" sticker had been plastered across the realty sign for at least two weeks and we were all dying to see our new neighbors. "Who are they?"

"I'm not sure, hon."

"Maybe they've got kids." I could feel the excitement in my stomach. Maybe a girl my age! A girl who would somehow magically become my best friend by the time school started so I'd never have to worry about Amy Higgins and Samantha McAllister again.

Dad snuck another piece of bacon and winked at me. I winked back.

"New kids would be so cool," I said, smiling as I pictured Amy trying to be best friends with me again while I was too busy with my new one, whoever she was.

"I saw a bike in the garage yesterday," Dad told me.

I smiled even wider at the thought. My new best friend and I could spend the rest of the summer cruising all over the neighborhood! I could show her my favorite spots, introduce her to everyone, and—

"A freestyle bike," Kenneth said, in his know-it-all way. "Definitely for dudes."

"Oh." My heart sank as the dream ended.

Just as I was about to drown my sorrows in orange juice, Grandma screamed.

Mom dropped the frying pan into the sink with a clatter and spun around. She looked even more scared than she did when Grandma had the stroke. "What is it?"

Grandma clamped one hand over her mouth, her dark brown eyes bulging, and used the other hand to point a shaking finger at Uncle Danny.

Judging by the scream, I was expecting to see that either his nose had fallen off his face or he was on fire.

Instead, aside from his scraggly new goatee, there was nothing to be alarmed about.

"Mom, what's wrong?" my mother asked Grandma.

Grandma uncovered her mouth and scowled at Uncle Danny. When she spoke, it was almost a growl—not the kind of voice you'd expect to hear from an old woman with a fluffy new perm. "I refuse to eat breakfast with a rat."

"Dora," my dad said, frowning at Grandma. "He's a lot of things, and not all of them good, but he's still my brother."

That was when I spotted the pair of beady brown eyes peering out from behind Uncle Danny's newspaper. "She means the ferret," I said.

"Good grief," Mom sighed, shaking her head. "Mom, you almost gave me a heart attack."

Grandma breathed through her nostrils like a bull about to charge and I hoped I hadn't picked the wrong day to wear a bright red T-shirt.

"I didn't spend seventy-five years on this earth to share a table with a dirty rodent," she said.

Uncle Danny carefully placed his hands over the ferret's ears, like it could understand that it was being insulted. "This isn't a rodent," he whispered. "Oliver is a highly intelligent creature who is going to make me a lot of money."

"Danny," Dad groaned. "Not another get-rich-quick scheme."

"No, no," Uncle Danny assured him.

My dad looked relieved for a second, until Uncle Danny added, "It won't be quick."

"Great. It sounds like hairless cats all over again," Dad muttered.

"The hairless ones were so rare, I thought . . ." Uncle Danny shrugged. "Well, how was I supposed to know that cat lovers prefer fur?"

"Common sense," I heard Mom say from the sink.

"And what about the mini lop-eared rabbits?" Dad asked.

"Hey, those are really big in Europe," Danny said.

Then why would they call them mini?

"Unfortunately, we're not in Europe," Dad reminded him. "How much did that business make, Dan?"

My uncle's expression was just like Clayton's when he flushed Dad's electric razor down the toilet.

"And I'm talking about the *profit* you made after all of your expenses were covered," Dad added.

"Well, when it was all said and done . . ." Uncle Danny licked his lips while we all waited for the answer. "I raked in about . . . twenty dollars."

"Or eleven," Kenneth whispered.

"And now we've moved on to ferrets," Dad said.

"Hey, every animal I've raised has been happy, healthy, and has gone to a good home."

"And now that home is mine," Mom sighed.

Before she could say anything more, a horn honked outside.

"That's Lindsay's mom, Callie," Mom said, waving at her through the window. "Don't keep her waiting."

I grabbed a slice of toast, piled my bacon and eggs onto it, then turned it into a sandwich by adding another slice on top and squishing it with the palm of my hand.

"That's disgusting," Kenneth said, taking another slurp of his cereal.

"You're the expert," I told him.

I stopped for a second to consider rinsing and loading my plate into the dishwasher. Lately I'd been wanting Mom and Dad to see that I wasn't a little kid anymore, that I was responsible. Then maybe they'd let me catch the bus to the aquatic center or the community pool for extra practice on the days Dad couldn't take me.

Mrs. Crisp honked again.

"Callie, what on earth are you waiting for?" Mom asked.

"Nothing," I said. I left my plate where it was and grabbed my backpack.

"Have fun," Mom and Dad both called after me.

I gave them a backward wave over my shoulder and jogged out to the minivan. Lindsay was in the front seat, and they'd already picked up Shannon and Katie, who both sat on the middle bench, giggling over some joke I was too late to hear.

The girls all went to Hoover Middle School, which meant I didn't know them as well as they knew one another. Mom worked with Mrs. Crisp, so the two of them had cooked up a bunch of field trips throughout the summer to keep us girls busy. I had a good time with them and everything, but I didn't feel like I belonged, the way I had with Amy.

"Hi, Callie," Shannon said through her giggles. I gave her a quick smile as I climbed into the van.

"I like your top," Katie said.

"Me too," Lindsay echoed.

"Thanks." It was one of my favorites.

"Ready to go?" Mrs. Crisp asked.

"Just a second," I told her, struggling to free my backpack strap from the armrest before looking toward the only seat left, in the very back of the van.

And there he sat, waiting for me.

Lars the German shepherd.

Great.

"Buckle up, please," Mrs. Crisp called back to me. I squeezed in next to The Beast and snapped my belt into place.

Lars licked my neck, and his tongue felt like a warm slug against my skin.

Ugh.

I tilted my head toward my shoulder so he couldn't do it again. Eating sideways was going to be interesting.

"Hey, what's that smell?" Lindsay asked from the front seat.

"It's *gross*," Shannon said, turning around to check out my break-fast sandwich, which had gotten even more squished since I'd put it together. A thin layer of grease made my thumb shine. "Eww! Is that *bacon?*"

"Yes," I said, lifting the sandwich toward my mouth.

"*Gross*," Katie said. "That's, like, pure fat."

A fact that Lars didn't seem to mind. He stared at my creation, his long pink tongue licking his chops. He was taller than me sit-ting down, and he looked hungry enough to eat not only my break-fast but my head.

In one bite.

It was a relief to know that he was a gentle giant and that the only rotten thing about poor old Lars was his breath.

Which was disgusting.

"You girls don't need to worry about fat," Mrs. Crisp said. "There's plenty of time for that kind of nonsense when you grow up. Just en-joy your childhood."

Yeah, right.

Why did adults always have to make it sound so easy to be a kid?

Chapter Three

Once we reached the outdoor pool, the girls and I made a beeline for the change room. Of all the places in the world (at least the ones I'd been to so far), I loved the smell of a pool's locker room the most. It was an almost perfect combination of chlorine, apple shampoo, and the baby powder older ladies sprinkled in their bathing caps.

I inhaled deeply for a moment, feeling like I was home.

Since we were already wearing our suits, we quickly stripped off our street clothes, tossed them into vacant cubbyholes, and headed for the shower, which was kind of like a metallic tree in the middle of a white tiled room. The sprays of warm water shooting out at all different heights were its branches.

Instead of a full shower, we stood under the water in our suits and flip-flops just long enough to rinse off before going outside to the pool.

The weatherman had been promising a heat wave all week, and since it was already warm, the place was packed with kids from all over the city. Some had come by bus, others with their parents, and some even took the train.

The coolest part about all of us being there together was that everywhere I looked I saw different colors of skin as arms, legs, and wet faces splashed in the water, like one big melting pot.

Along with all of the different shades of people, I loved the bright flashes of the bathing suits, as more kids jumped in the water.

The melting pot was a very busy place.

There was a game of Marco Polo going on in the deep end, and some girls about our age jumped into the water midway down the pool. Babies with floatie wings tried to paddle across the shallow end, laughing while their moms coaxed them closer and closer to the concrete edge with singsong voices. I imagined my dad did the same thing when I first learned to swim.

I smiled.

There really wasn't anything in the world I loved more than a pool.

Whenever Dad had a day off from the bank, he took me to the Sunnyridge aquatic center for the early morning session. It was big, new, and the only place nearby that we could swim in all year round. He helped me practice my strokes and taught me some of the easier dives he knew. He'd been the captain of his college diving team when he was young (and skinny) and he'd always loved it. He was good, too. I knew because I'd stumbled across some dusty trophies in the garage once, but he never bragged about them.

He wasn't that kind of guy.

Since Kenneth hadn't been seen in trunks for about three years (and the glare of his pasty white skin could probably cause temporary blindness) and Clay was too young, it was just me and Dad on those mornings. It was hard to say what I liked most about going with him, because I loved having him all to myself almost as much as the diving.

He was always patient with me and whenever I messed up, he encouraged me to try again by saying, "I know you'll make it. After all, you're Callie Boone." It was something I'd heard from him over and over again for as long as I could remember, whether I was learning to ride my bike without training wheels or struggling with math homework.

I know you'll make it. After all, you're Callie Boone.

Sometimes I believed him, and sometimes I wasn't so sure, but I always liked to hear it.

It might seem kind of silly, but when I wasn't in the pool, I loved to daydream about someday being on the high school diving team and maybe even getting a diving scholarship for college. Imagining the look on my dad's face if I won a big competition and a trophy of my own always gave me goose bumps.

Of course, I'd never told anyone (not even Amy) about the scholarship daydream. I figured they'd call me crazy for thinking I could become that good, that fast. After all, I was already eleven and I'd only just started.

An even deeper secret was that I often imagined I was at the medals ceremony for the Olympics. I could see myself as an older teenager, wearing a team tracksuit covered in stars and stripes with my name on the back, bowing my head as they placed the silver (okay, gold) medal around my neck. Tears would stream down my cheeks as Dad cheered from the stands. We would sing along with the national anthem, knowing we'd made it there together.

That was the most thrilling thing about our morning practices. With Dad guiding me, I felt like each lap and dive was bringing me closer to that dream. It made me want to try as hard as I possibly could.

Even though I hated the laps.

Swimming at the community pool was a totally different story, though. When I was there, I just goofed around and played games like everyone else so I wouldn't look like a show-off.

No one likes a show-off.

Shannon, Katie, Lindsay, and I draped our towels over the chain-link fence for later. Mrs. Crisp had settled into a lounge chair under a shady tree and was nose deep in a paperback mystery, paying no attention to what we were doing.

Unfortunately for us, the pool had a lifeguard to do that.

His name was Andy, and every girl but me thought he was cute. They were always trying to get his attention, even pretending they couldn't swim very well, hoping he might jump in and save them. It was ludicrous (one of my favorite words). To me, he was just the bossy guy in the oversized high chair who spent half his time yelling at everybody for running on deck and the other half flirting with teenage girls in bikinis.

When I looked at the older girls with their long hair and perfect bodies, it was hard to imagine that I could ever be like them. Most of the girls I knew were anxious to get boobs and all that junk, but I wasn't looking forward to any of it. Teenagers seemed to spend most of their time trying to look good *around* the pool instead of having fun *in* it.

I knew for a fact that no matter how old I got, I'd rather be swimming.

Boobs and boys?

Who needed them?

That was probably the worst part about losing Amy. When it came to not caring about that stuff, she was exactly like me.

At least I'd *thought* she was, until Samantha McAllister stole her away with stupid sparkly makeup and endless boy talk.

It was revolting (another one of my favorites).

"Callie, are you coming in, or what?" Shannon called from the edge of the pool.

Lindsay and Katie were already playing Marco Polo, so I met Shannon at the stairs. I dipped my toes into the perfectly cool water.

During my mornings with Dad, we always counted down "one for the money, two for the show," before leaping into the water, but I sometimes liked to ease in slowly, letting my body get used to the temperature and watching the bumps on my arms pop up, then disappear.

Shannon and I inched down the steps, talking about our favorite movies, until we were waist deep. At that point, we each took a deep breath and dove in.

Just like always, it felt perfect.

I loved the way the world was totally silent underwater. I was so happy down there, I actually hummed to myself, my voice sounding thick and muffled in my head. I loved the way all of my movements slowed down, and the way everything that would have been clumsy and awkward on the ground was pretty and graceful under the surface.

When I came up for air, my ears popped and all of the splashing kids sounded louder than ever.

Shannon and I swam over to the Marco Polo group and pretty soon everyone who could handle the deep end was playing. I didn't see anyone from school, but I recognized a few kids from earlier visits to the pool. It was so much fun, I almost forgot about how much I missed Amy.

Almost.

Around noon, Mrs. Crisp called us over for lunch, which was okay because I was starving and my skin was all pruned up. She'd packed peanut butter sandwiches, juice boxes, and apples for us, so we had our picnic in the shade, then laid on our towels in the warm sun. It didn't take long before we were too hot and had to head back into the pool.

Shannon took off her sport watch and dropped it in the water so we could swim all the way to the bottom to get it. We kept diving for it, starting fairly shallow, then moving closer and closer toward the deep end.

I turned out to be the best at holding my breath, and by the time we reached the deepest end of the pool, I was the only one who could still get the watch.

"You're a really good swimmer, Callie," Lindsay told me, treading water and smiling.

"Thanks," I said, pleased that she thought so.

"Do you have a pool at home?" Shannon asked.

"I wish!" Now *that* would be a dream come true. I'd probably sleep on a raft every night (at least until school started), floating around under the stars. A real waterbed.

"But you're *so* good," Lindsay said.

"Thanks," I said again, feeling flattered.

"Yeah, you're awesome," Katie added.

I couldn't help smiling, but didn't know what to say. After all, I wasn't one to brag, but I *was* pretty good.

"Do you take lessons?" Lindsay asked.

"No," I said, almost laughing at the idea. I hadn't taken lessons for years.

I didn't know if I wanted to tell them about practicing with

Dad. Ever since Amy ditched me, I wasn't sure which things that I thought were normal might seem weird or stupid to other kids, but after thinking about it, I decided to spill the beans.

"My dad's kind of training me."

"For what?" Katie asked.

I wanted to say, "The Olympics," but I just smiled and said, "For fun." I explained that he'd been a great swimmer and diver when he was young.

"Cool," Shannon said. "Can you do any dives?"

"A couple," I said, not wanting to show off.

Actually, it was more like five, although my form and entry on all of them could still use some work.

"Can we see?" Lindsay asked.

"What, here?" I asked, caught off guard.

"Yeah," Katie said.

Oh, fish sticks.

There were way too many people around!

"Uh . . . I don't know."

What I did know was that I should have kept my mouth shut.

"Come on, Callie. Just one dive," Shannon said. "It would be really cool."

"*Super* cool," Katie agreed. "Especially if you do it from the diving board."

Diving board?

I thought they meant something more like a quickie from the pool deck. "I'm not sure that's a good idea."

"You *can* do it, right?" Lindsay asked, frowning. "I mean, you weren't just making up the stuff about being in training, were you?"

"No!" I felt my cheeks get hot.

Had I said "in training"? That sounded much more . . . formal than my practices with Dad.

"I want to see," Shannon said. "Come on, Callie."

"Yeah, just show us," Katie added.

With all three asking to see me dive, it wasn't long before I was pulling myself out of the pool and walking toward the short board, leaving a trail of water behind me on the warm concrete deck.

With every step, I felt my stomach tighten while a butterfly fluttered in my chest. I'd never dove for a real audience before, and the idea of everyone watching me had me feeling nervous . . . but also kind of proud and excited.

I walked past Andy the lifeguard, who was too busy talking to a blond girl to notice me.

So far, so good.

I started to climb the two steps of the short board, anxious to get it over with, but saw the girls shaking their heads and pointing at the big one.

What?

"You can do it!" Shannon shouted.

The fluttering in my chest turned to pounding, like the butterflies wanted to break free and fly away.

The high diving board wasn't what I'd signed up for.

The idea of trying to do something cool enough to impress the girls from way up there was kind of scary.

Okay, *really* scary.

I stopped at the base of the ladder for a second and saw the girls grinning and cheering me on.

The sign right in front of me said: "No Children."

I gulped.

Get a grip on yourself.

I took a deep breath and gave it some thought.

The fact was, I'd managed to do a few simple forward dives from the high board with Dad before. I could handle that. And considering the only thing I'd ever seen anyone do at the outdoor pool was a cannonball that soaked almost everybody on deck, I figured that even something easy would be impressive.

What could go wrong?

Nothing.

Right?

I started climbing the ladder, and with each step, I grew a tiny bit more confident. After all, it wasn't like I was going to do something I'd never done before. I started to hear the familiar buzz of excitement in my ears and kept climbing.

It's not really *that* high.

There's nothing to worry about.

"Hey!" a man's voice shouted from below.

I glanced down and saw Andy the lifeguard standing on his tower.

I froze.

"Hey, little girl, you can't go up there!"

Little girl?

All of a sudden, every face both in the pool and out of it was pointed in my direction.

Staring.

Did he actually think I'd climb down with everybody watching me?

If I didn't, would he carry me down himself?

Oh, fish sticks.

Obviously, the only way to get out of the situation without dying of embarrassment was to keep climbing and pull off a really good dive.

This was getting complicated.

When I moved to the next step, I heard Andy blow his whistle, but I kept going.

There was nothing else I *could* do.

"Get down from there," his voice boomed through a megaphone.

I kept climbing, my hope turning into determination that I could somehow wow the crowd.

I heard the people below me chattering excitedly, like monkeys at the zoo. When I reached the board itself, I was shaking both with nerves and the thrill of being up there as the center of attention.

Dad (and whoever happened to be taking a break from laps to watch us at Sunnyridge) was the only person who'd ever watched me, and suddenly I had a big audience rooting for me.

It was the closest I'd ever been to my Olympic dream.

"Get down, now!" Andy shouted.

I scanned the crowd and saw that Mrs. Crisp had dropped her paperback to stare up at me. Even from that height, I recognized her expression as horrified, but that wasn't enough to stop me.

After all, her horror was about to turn into amazement.

I pictured myself completing the dive, with a tidy, tiny splash, just like Dad had taught me to do. He called it "visualization." As I walked toward the end of the board, I could practically hear his voice saying, "I know you'll make it. After all, you're Callie Boone."

When I looked down again, the people in the pool seemed so far away! The girls were waving at me and shouting something I couldn't hear over all the other noise.

Andy was out of his tower and running down the deck toward

my ladder. He looked angrier than Mom did when Clayton colored her wedding photos with permanent ink.

In all of the excitement, it hadn't crossed my mind that I might get in serious trouble for making the dive.

That is, until Andy started climbing the ladder.

I took a deep breath and began counting off my steps to the end of the board. I concentrated as hard as I could and, with each step, I felt a little stronger and more prepared. My visualization got even better as I imagined everyone congratulating me when I got out of the pool, patting me on the back and telling me how incredible my dive had been.

I can do this.

With just four steps left before the end of the board, I briefly broke my concentration to take one more quick look at my cheering fans.

Bad idea.

There they were.

Amy Higgins and Samantha McAllister stood at the door to the change room, pointing at me . . . and laughing.

I almost froze, but then heard Andy's voice close behind me. "Get off the board, kid!"

There was no time for me to take a final breath or "visualize" the dive again. All I could do was go for it.

So I did.

The moment I was in the air, I knew that my positioning was all wrong.

My arms and legs seemed to be doing whatever they wanted, instead of what I told them to, and it was only a couple of seconds before I hit the water.

When I hit the surface, it wasn't a clean entry, like the knife into water Dad always talked about.

It was a big fat belly flop.

And it hurt.

The sting I felt on every square inch of my body was painful, but it was only half as bad as the burn of embarrassment.

What had I done?

I only had a second or two of perfect silence underwater before I had to come up for air. When I did, instead of hearing the thunder of applause from my audience, I heard the deafening roar of laughter.

And then a red-faced, hopping-mad Andy banned me from the pool.

Permanently.

Chapter Four

I didn't say much on the ride home, but it didn't matter because everyone else was doing the talking . . . and laughing. Shannon, Lindsay, and Katie relived my dive at least four times, each version more dramatic and "comical" than the last.

They thought it was hilarious and harmless, and they wanted me to join in, like I normally did when we joked around.

But it wasn't funny to me.

At all.

Mrs. Crisp was silent, but her white-knuckled grip on the steering wheel and the dirty looks she kept shooting me in the rearview mirror said plenty.

Lars, the German shepherd, was too busy with a punctured rubber hot dog to even look at me, so at least I didn't have to defend myself against his slobbery tongue.

Instead I just stared out the window.

I felt like such an idiot. No matter how hard I tried, I couldn't come up with a way to undo what I'd done.

Banned from the pool!

Humiliated in front of a huge crowd of people.

The only silver lining was that I wouldn't see most of those kids again, but even that didn't matter. I knew once school started, the story was going to spread anyway, courtesy of my former best friend, Amy Higgins.

It was a sickening feeling, knowing that the person who knew me better than anyone (even my parents) wasn't on my side anymore.

I felt kind of hollowed out, like whatever she said about me would be enough to knock me to the ground.

I closed my eyes and wished my dad would get transferred so we could move to Iowa . . . or another planet.

If I could start my whole life over somewhere else, I wouldn't have to deal with this mess.

When we pulled into my driveway and I started to quietly climb out of the van, things didn't get any better.

"Callie," Mrs. Crisp said in a tired voice, "tell your mother that I'd like her to call me this evening."

"I will," I said.

My face felt warm, so I knew it was bright red.

Again.

"We have some things to discuss," she said.

As if I didn't know that.

My head started to hurt, thinking of all the things Mrs. Crisp might say to Mom.

The other girls stopped chattering long enough to say good-bye, and their happy, carefree smiles made me feel even worse.

"Cheer up, Callie. It's not that bad," Shannon said.

"No big deal," Lindsay agreed, while Katie gave me a smile of encouragement. "It was funny."

Funny?

Of course, *they* didn't have anything to worry about. Even

though they were the ones who'd encouraged me to dive, and it was partly their fault that I was in trouble, *I* was the only one who'd have to face the wrath of Sergeant Boone in my very own kitchen.

The whole situation stunk.

The van pulled away, and with each of my heavy steps toward the front door, my driveway felt more and more like a flower-lined path to death row.

"Hey."

A boy about my age, with shaggy brown hair, stood on the other side of our hedge.

The new kid.

At first I thought his face was splattered with dirt, but when I looked closer I saw it was actually sprinkled with freckles.

"Hey," he repeated with a smile. He was wearing a T-shirt that was just like one of Kenneth's, covered with fish skeletons and words that looked like graffiti.

Total skateboarder.

I wasn't exactly in the mood for chitchat, so I kept walking. I knew it was rude, but I didn't care.

"You live here?" he asked in a raspy voice.

"Well, duh," I muttered.

He laughed. "'Well, duh' is the best you can do?"

I turned to glare at him.

Who did he think he was anyway?

"Man, if someone asked a question that dumb back in Philly, they'd get burned by a comeback so fast, they wouldn't know what hit 'em."

"Philly?" I asked, annoyed that he'd baited me into it.

He laughed again and shook his head like he couldn't believe I didn't know what he was talking about. "Philadelphia. My home-town."

"Oh," I said, feeling foolish.

"In Philly, someone would have said something like—"

"This isn't Philly," I snapped.

"Well, *duh*," he said, laughing harder. "Are you the only kid here?"

I sighed loudly, hoping he'd get the idea that I had better things to do than spend my whole stinking afternoon yacking in the drive-way with some strange boy.

"Brothers?" he asked. "Sisters?"

"Two brothers."

"How old are they?" he asked, hopefully.

"Fifteen and three," I was pleased to report.

Instead of looking disappointed, like he should have, he kept smiling. "Cool. So, who's the old lady in the nightgown?"

Grandma had gone outside in her nightie *again*?

Oh, fish sticks and tartar!

"My grandma."

"She's . . . pretty interesting."

"You were talking to her?"

Could this day get any worse?

Wasn't there some way I could hide in my bedroom until I was forty?

"No, I was just watching her. Does she live with you?"

I stared at him, trying to copy Kenneth's most exasperated look. "Are you a reporter or something?"

"No, why?"

"Because you've asked me about a million questions."

"Nice math skills," he said, laughing yet again. "More like three or four."

"You know what I mean," I snapped.

Man, was he pushing my buttons.

He shrugged. "How else am I supposed to find stuff out?" He pulled a pack of gum from the pocket of his jeans and offered me a piece. When I shook my head, he pushed a red square through the foil and popped it into his mouth. "By the way, does anything happen around here?"

"Like what?" All I could smell was cinnamon.

"Like anything. So far, it seems like the West Coast is more like the *Rest* Coast. Where's all the action?"

I cringed.

At the community pool.

"Haven't you been here, like, one day?" I asked, growing even more irritated. Before he could answer, I told him, "Look, I've got to go inside, okay?" I started toward the door again.

He wasn't finished yet. "I'm Hoot, by the way."

I couldn't help turning around. "You're *who*?"

"No, Hoot." He grinned, then blew a big bubble. I was glad when it popped in his face and he had to scrape it off his chin with his fingernails.

Despite my foul mood, I was curious.

"Hoot, like an owl?" I asked.

"No, like a guy from Philly who wants someone to show him around the neighborhood." He paused to wiggle his eyebrows at me. "Hint, hint."

I stopped and stared at him. "What, you mean me?"

"Why not?" He shrugged. "You're about my age."

"I'm eleven."

"Cool. I'm twelve. So, it's a plan."

I nearly choked. "No, it isn't."

He slapped his forehead. "You're right! A plan has a time and place attached to it. Okay, we'll meet right here, tomorrow at ten."

"But I—"

"What's your name?"

"Callie, but—"

He scrunched up his face and half the freckles disappeared into the creases. "Callie-butt?"

Oh, brother.

I sighed. "No, just Callie."

"Nice to meet ya, Callie. See you tomorrow."

And with that, he stepped away from the hedge and into his garage.

I slowly walked toward my front door, wondering just what I'd gotten myself into and, more important, how I'd done it.

Hoot?

Between my new, weird neighbor and the disaster at the pool, the day had sucked everything out of me. All I could do was sigh as I entered the house.

Thankfully, no one was home but Grandma, who sat on the couch, watching *Oprah*.

"Care to join me?" she asked, patting the cushion next to her.

"Sure." I dropped my backpack in the hallway with a thud and flopped on the couch.

Sometimes I wished we were a normal family (well, more normal anyway), with just kids and parents living in the house, like everyone else I knew. At other times, like that particular moment, I appreciated Grandma's company.

Before she moved in with us, I only saw Grandma a couple of

times a month, and that was with the whole gang of us crammed into her living room, all talking at the same time.

After the stroke, she recovered completely, but the doctors didn't want her to live alone anymore, just in case.

Once she settled in down the hall from my bedroom, we had plenty of time to spend together, just the two of us. The bad part was that she did almost all of the talking and was usually a bit too focused on the TV, but it was nice to sit and listen to her opinions on talk shows or soaps. (Well, sometimes anyway.) She groaned at the commercials, and every now and then she told me she'd teach me how to knit someday.

I didn't really want to learn, but I guess it was nice of her to think of it.

When Oprah took a commercial break, Grandma nudged me with a bony elbow. "Rough day?"

"Yes." It seemed like the perfect opportunity to tell her all about how unfair life was, and I was gearing up to do just that, when she beat me to the punch.

"Me too. This arthritis is killing me."

"Oh," I said. Arthritis? I was already outmatched. "Sorry, Grandma."

"Hey, it's not your fault I've got grumpy old bones. Never mind the fact that I haven't slept a wink since those nasty creatures moved into the house."

Nasty creatures?

"The ferrets?" I asked. "You know, technically, the garage isn't *in* the house."

She gave me a doubtful look, then turned back to the TV. "What, you think they can't squeeze in through the ducts?"

"They're in cages, Grandma."

"Hmph." She crossed her arms and frowned at an air freshener commercial, then relaxed when Oprah came back on the screen. She didn't say a word, other than the occasional "You got that right" when Oprah made a point, until the next set of commercials.

"So, what's got you so mopey?" she asked.

Great, she was only giving me a two-minute window to tell the whole story.

I took a deep breath. I knew from loads of experience that she wasn't the cute and cuddly kind of grandma other kids had, baking cookies and hugging everybody, but I needed to talk anyway. Hopefully, she'd say something to make me feel better, or even just . . . listen. "Things got a little out of control at—"

"When I was your age, the whole world was at war, and we didn't have time for moping."

"Oh." I had the sneaking suspicion that my story about the mess at the pool wasn't going to get much sympathy.

"I didn't taste chocolate for *three years*, Callie."

I wasn't sure what she was talking about, but that was nothing new. I nodded as though I understood and told her I was sorry to hear it.

I seemed to spend a lot of time telling Grandma I was sorry.

She told me about all of the older boys shipping out and never coming home again, and how scared she'd been that her own brothers would be sent to fight.

With every word, I shrank a little more in my seat, slowly realizing that there was no way on earth I could tell Grandma my life was ruined because Amy Higgins didn't like me anymore and I'd embarrassed myself with a belly flop at the community pool.

It totally stunk.

When her show came back on, I told Grandma I'd see her at dinner, then carried my backpack up to my room to unload it.

While I put my things away, I tried to do what Dad always suggested when I was feeling down. I looked for silver linings.

Naturally, I couldn't think of a single one right off the bat, so I lay on my bed and stared at the ceiling, hoping for inspiration.

It took some time, but eventually I came up with a couple of things that might not have been silver, but maybe bronze.

One was that there was a good chance that something more gossip-worthy than my belly flop would happen in the several weeks before school started. The other was that my public humiliation was a onetime thing, and if I wanted to, I could practice diving to the point that nothing would ever distract me on the diving board again.

Not even Amy.

By dinnertime, I was almost back to my old self.

That is, until Kenneth opened his big mouth.

He was passing me the peas, when he asked, "So, who's your new boyfriend?"

Oh, fish sticks.

He must have seen me talking to Hoot.

Everyone at the table stopped what they were doing.

Dad raised his eyebrows, Mom smiled uncertainly, Uncle Danny stirred his peas into his potatoes, and Grandma just stared at me. Of course, Clayton was too busy talking to his chicken nuggets to pay much attention.

"Boyfriend?" Mom asked, frowning.

"I don't know what you're talking about," I told my big brother. I tried to concentrate on balancing as many peas on my fork as I could while I felt my face turning red, yet again. I could vaguely remember a time when I looked up to Kenneth, but of course that was before he became a king-sized jerk.

"Your new skater guy," he said with a smirk, "next door."

"He's not my skater guy."

"So, there *is* a boy," Mom said, glancing at Dad.

"No!" A couple of peas fell off the fork. "I mean, yes, but Hoot's not my boyfriend."

"Hoot?" Grandma asked. "What kind of a name is that?"

"Australian?" Uncle Danny asked.

What?

"It's probably a nickname," I told the table, wishing they'd drop the subject.

"Is he your age?" Dad asked.

"He's twelve," I sighed.

"An *older* man," Uncle Danny said in a teasing voice.

Couldn't they all just leave me alone?

"Look, I only met him today and I'm showing him around the neighborhood tomorrow."

"Sounds like a date," Kenneth said, snorting. "Very interesting."

"Not really," Grandma said. "What's interesting is the gal Oprah had on today. She was thirty-seven years old and she'd been in a terrible car accident."

I silently thanked her, then stopped listening while she described the show.

As I chewed on a piece of pork, I could only think about one thing. If my own family was having a field day with the idea of me hanging out with a boy, what would the other kids do if they saw us around the neighborhood together?

The last thing I needed was more negative attention.

But it wasn't like I had any control over it.

Suddenly, I wasn't hungry.

I excused myself from the table as soon as I could and carried my almost-full plate into the kitchen.

Dad followed me. "You okay, kiddo?"

When I heard his gentle voice, all I wanted to do was cry over everything that seemed to be going wrong at once, but I held back.

Just like Grandma living through a war, I knew Dad's troubles were way bigger than mine. His job was making the final decisions on whether or not the bank should loan people money for houses and stuff like that. It seemed like every day he had to upset really nice people by telling them no.

My problems would sound stupid compared to that.

And I was sick of stupid.

"I'm fine," I told him, sounding surprisingly calm. "Just a bit tired, I guess."

He looked at me for a long time, like we were in a staring contest.

"Okay," he finally said, but I could tell he wasn't convinced. "Why don't you have a quiet night, maybe take a book upstairs and read?"

It actually sounded like the perfect idea, mainly because it would give me some time to brainstorm a way out of my "plans" with Hoot in the morning. I couldn't do anything about the mess at the pool, but at least Amy and Samantha wouldn't have *him* to tease me about.

"Sounds good," I told Dad.

"And Saturday morning, we practice," he added. "Right?"

I thought about the cool, clear water at the aquatic center, where only seniors who were too busy worrying about wrinkles and vitamins to pay much attention to me would be around.

I could definitely handle that.

"Right!"

When I got to my room, I was ready to come up with the perfect plan to avoid Hoot, but I started to feel kind of bad about him instead.

The truth was, even though he'd annoyed me, he seemed like a nice, friendly boy. And I couldn't imagine moving to a new city where I didn't know a single person.

What if I tried to make friends and the first person I met was a ball of snot, like I'd been?

Dad always said it was important to be kind to other people, and thinking of that made me feel even worse.

But I knew I had to protect myself from the teasing that came from hanging out with a boy.

Even a nice one.

The more I thought about it, the more I knew I needed an excuse, so I finally settled on a big fat lie. When Kenneth was grounded for lighting firecrackers in the kitchen, he couldn't go outside or have friends over for two whole weeks.

Perfect.

Sorry, Hoot. I'm grounded.

Once the decision was made, I breathed a sigh of relief.

That is, until Mom shouted from the kitchen, "Callie Anne Boone, get down here this instant!"

I leaped out of bed, knowing from experience that a speedy response was the only kind Mom accepted. I ran down the stairs, losing one sock on the way, and made it to the kitchen in a matter of seconds.

Mom was standing next to the fridge, one hand on her hip, the other resting on the phone, which she'd apparently just hung up. Her expression was hard to read. Her piercing eyes were angry, but her thin, tightened lips leaned more toward disappointment.

"Hi," I said cheerfully, as though nothing was wrong.

"Hi," she said. Her jaw pulsed.

Definitely angry.

"Mrs. Crisp just called."

The back of my neck got all prickly.

Uh-oh.

"She said you were supposed to tell me to call her."

"I forgot," I told her. Between Grandma, Oprah, the war, three years without chocolate, and my new "boyfriend," I had honestly forgotten all about Mrs. Crisp.

"I see," Mom said. "So, it sounds like you had a pretty busy day at the pool."

"I guess," I said very, very quietly.

"Disobeying the lifeguard? Ignoring the rules? What were you thinking?"

If I'd been thinking, it wouldn't have happened.

"If you'd been thinking, it wouldn't have happened, Callie."

Great, Mom had X-ray vision and she could read minds. She must be a superhero.

"I'm sorry," I told her. I was sorrier about that stupid dive than she'd ever know.

"Not as sorry as I am." She sighed and rubbed her forehead. "Mrs. Crisp says she can't take you out with the girls anymore."

"What?" I gasped.

Those outings were the only good part of my summer!

"She said having an uncontrollable child with her was too much to handle."

It wasn't fair. I always followed the rules and did what I was supposed to. Just because I made one lousy mistake, I wasn't going to get a second chance?

"I'm not uncontrollable!"

"You were today." Her nostrils flared.

"But those girls made me do it!"

She shook her head slowly from side to side, swinging back to disappointment. "No one can make you do anything, Callie."

That wasn't true! Mom could make me go straight to my room with no chance to explain myself.

Which was exactly what she did.

Chapter Five

By the time morning rolled around, I felt like I hadn't slept at all, which just might be the most rotten feeling on earth (aside from your best friend dumping you for no good reason or your older brother licking his finger, sticking it in your ear, and wiggling it around in there until you were ready to scream).

I laid in bed, listening to the usual racket of Mom and Dad getting ready for work, Clayton chatting with more of his breakfast than he ate, and Kenneth taking the longest shower in the history of the universe while Grandma banged on the door because it was time to take her pills, which were in the medicine cabinet.

I need to add earplugs to my birthday wish list.

When it sounded like the coast was clear, I rolled out of bed and went downstairs to make some cinnamon toast and find the note I was sure Mom had taped to the fridge door for me.

There it was, right at eye level. No surprise, considering she wasn't the kind of person who left things hanging (other than notes anyway).

It said: *"Callie, I'd like you to get some chores done around the house today. Please unload the dishwasher, fold what you can of the* laundry (I'll do the sheets), take the ground turkey out of the freezer to defrost for dinner, set the table, and help Grandma wash her hair if she needs you. Love, Mom. P.S. We aren't finished talking about the pool incident."

Great.

I ate my cinnamon toast while reading the newspaper comics, then unloaded the dishwasher and started on the laundry. I was right in the middle of matching endless pairs of socks when the doorbell rang.

Instead of answering it, Grandma turned up the volume on the TV in the living room so she wouldn't miss a word of her soap opera.

Rolling my eyes, I dropped the loose socks back into the laundry basket. I only wondered who might be at the door for a second before I saw the kitchen clock.

I'd completely forgotten about Hoot!

More important, I'd forgotten to practice the "grounded" lie I'd planned to send his way.

I ran to the front door, half relieved that Mom had left me the chores. Even though folding and defrosting probably wouldn't make the highlight reel of my life, at least I had a solid excuse not to hang out with the new kid.

I opened the door, and there he was, wearing another skateboard T-shirt, dark blue cargo shorts at least two sizes too big for him, and a pair of Vans that were made up almost entirely of holes. A bicycle leaned against his hip.

I caught a whiff of his cinnamon gum.

"How's it going?" he asked, looking my pink-and-green striped pajamas up and down with a laugh. "Running late?"

"No, I—"

"I brought my bike," he said, squeezing the brakes and pushing the back tire into the air. "This seems like a good neighborhood for riding."

"It is, but—"

"But what?" he asked, tilting his head. He had dark brown eyes like a puppy's.

Heartlessly ditching him was going to be harder than I thought.

I cleared my throat, but not my conscience.

"I, uh . . . can't go."

He stared at me for a second. "Why not?"

Yeah, why not?

Because if we're seen together, I'd never live it down.

"Well, there was this . . . *thing* at the pool yesterday, my mom's punishing me with indoor chores, and—"

"I'll help," he said with a shrug.

"What?" I gasped.

"I'll help. We'll get it done in half the time and then we can take off."

I was about to toss out another lie and say that I wasn't allowed to let anyone in the house, when Grandma shouted from the living room, "Who's out there, Callie?"

"The boy next door. He's just—"

"Well, invite him in, for crying out loud. You're letting all the cold air out. Today's supposed to be a scorcher."

Hoot smiled and rested his bike against the house before walking inside.

There was nothing I could do.

Thanks, Grandma.

I introduced the two of them, more than a little worried about what totally embarrassing thing Grandma might say. She could be counted on to blab about how I used to pile all my stuffed animals around my head at night so they could protect me from monsters, with no warning.

Hoot gave her a nice handshake and called her ma'am, which meant Grandma fell in love with him on the spot.

"Well, aren't you a nice young man," she said, shooting me a rare smile of approval.

"Thank you," Hoot said, looking down at his hand like he might want her to let go of it sometime in the next week or so.

Luckily, her commercial break ended and she was too distracted by her show to say anything more.

I led the way into the kitchen.

"So, where do we start?" Hoot asked.

I couldn't figure him out. "Why do you want to do this?" I asked, hands on my hips, just like Mom.

"Hello?" he asked, gently knocking his knuckles on the top of my head, like it was hollow. "So we can ride bikes."

"There are other kids around here who could—"

"Yeah, but you're right next door and I like you."

"What?" I felt my face turning red.

"Do you need a hearing aid, Callie?" He laughed.

"No, it's just that . . . you don't even know me."

"Big deal." He shrugged again. "My mom always says that first impressions count."

"But I—"

"When I saw how ticked off you looked when you got out of that minivan yesterday, I liked you right away."

I stared at him. "Really?" I stared even harder when he nodded. "But why?"

"I don't know. I could just tell you weren't some prissy girl." He shook his head. "I can't stand prissy girls."

"Me neither," I said, thinking of the bikini teens at the pool who never swam because they were afraid their perfect hair or makeup would be ruined.

For the first time since I'd met him, I smiled at Hoot.

"So, where do we start?" he asked again.

I showed him the list and he snorted with laughter. "That's your mom's idea of chores? Mine gives me a *whole page* at a time. Man, your mom must be pretty nice."

"Actually, she's a drill sergeant," I told him. "Or was, anyway. She teaches at the college now."

"Wow," Hoot said. "I've never met a lady drill sergeant. Do you think she—"

"*Ex*-drill sergeant," I reminded him. "It was a long time ago."

"Too bad," Hoot said with a shrug. "I think it's pretty cool." He ran a sponge under the faucet, then dug underneath the sink for some cleaning supplies. Before I knew it, he was scrubbing the countertops.

"Mom didn't say I had to—"

"But won't she be happy if you do?" He gave me a lopsided grin.

"I guess, but—"

"Happy enough that she might forget about the thing?"

"Thing?" I asked, pulling out the place mats to set the table.

"The thing at the pool."

"Oh." My stomach sank.

"What was it, anyway?"

I watched him squirt the cleaning liquid and scrub some more. I'd barely met him, but he seemed nice, he was helping me, *and* he didn't have anyone to tell, so I gave him a brief description of the belly flop. When I finished, he was laughing so hard he started coughing.

"It's not funny," I snapped.

"Sure it is."

"No, Hoot. It isn't."

His laughter slowed down, but didn't stop entirely. "Geez, what are you so freaked out about?"

"Everyone's going to know." My eyes stung, but the thought of crying in front of this strange boy was embarrassing enough to make me cringe instead.

"So what?"

I took a deep breath and told him about how badly things were going for me, especially the part about Amy.

I hadn't said anything about my ex-best friend to anyone, but for some reason, it was easy to talk to Hoot.

He stood still and listened as I told him all about what great friends we'd been until the day she started spending every stupid second with Samantha McAllister instead. He nodded slowly when I told him that she'd never even said *why* she didn't like me anymore, or what I'd done to make everything change. I managed to tell the whole story without crying, and was kind of proud of myself for that.

When I finished, he didn't say anything for a couple of minutes.

That was almost enough to drive me crazy.

Then he started on the countertop again.

"Well?" I finally asked.

"Well, what?" He looked over at me, confused.

"I just told you that big long story, and it was really hard for me to do, and now you aren't saying *anything.*"

He frowned. "What do you want me to say?"

It was my turn to rap my knuckles on his head. "Hello? What you think about it, I guess."

"Well," he said, running the water over his sponge again and squeezing it dry. "She doesn't sound like a friend to me." He shrugged. "Friends don't do that."

The first thing I wanted to do was defend her. She was my friend, for almost my whole life. But when I opened my mouth to say something, I couldn't come up with a single defense for Amy.

After all, even *I* didn't understand what had happened.

While Hoot found a broom and started sweeping the tile floor, I just stood there.

He was right.

Friends didn't do that. They didn't like you one day and ignore you the next, or say rotten things about you and act like you weren't cool enough for them. They were supposed to like you whether you wanted to talk about boys all day or not.

I never would have done what Amy did to me.

As he worked, I just stared into space, thinking about it.

The more I thought, the more I felt that friends were supposed to be like your family. Clayton could be a huge pain in the butt, but I still *loved* him. Kenneth and I fought sometimes, but we always made up. And so what if Grandma spent most of her time in a nightie? She was old, she lived through a war, and she just wanted to be comfortable.

Big deal.

I thought some more about Amy.

That sick feeling returned to my stomach. I missed seeing her every day and felt horribly embarrassed whenever I thought of the conversation I overheard that day at school or the ferret incident in the front yard.

But I actually felt a little bit better, too.

Of course, it still hurt and I still wished we were best friends, but somehow I didn't feel quite as lonely as I did before talking to Hoot.

I finished folding the laundry, humming to myself. I didn't even make an awful face when I had to touch Kenneth's underwear.

And that was saying something.

Hoot and I spent an hour cleaning. We mopped the floor, took out the garbage, and even straightened up as much of the living room as we could, although Grandma said that under no circumstances were we to turn on the vacuum during *The Price Is Right*. When I offered to help with her hair, she said she could handle it.

By the time we finished, I felt really good, knowing how surprised and happy Mom would be to come home and find everything looking so nice.

Thanks to Hoot, I was one step closer to being seen as a responsible kid.

"Grandma, me and Hoot are going for a bike ride," I told her, when all the cleaning supplies were put away, the house practically sparkled, and I'd traded my pajamas for regular clothes.

"Come here," she said.

Uh-oh.

I walked over to the couch and she grabbed my hand with her cold, bony fingers. She looked into my eyes as she pressed a piece of paper into my palm. "You're a good girl, Callie. Have a treat on me."

I looked down and saw a ten-dollar bill.

"Thank you," I said, stunned.

I could already smell the waffle cones at Sweet Dreams. Ten dollars was enough for double scoops for both of us, *and* money left over.

I tucked the money into my sock and zipped through the side

door to the garage alone so I could pull my red mountain bike and helmet out front without Hoot seeing the ferrets.

I *really* didn't feel like explaining them.

Once we hit the road, Hoot was all over the place, racing ahead, then doing mini-jumps off the curb or popping wheelies. I would have thought he was showing off, but he didn't seem to care if anybody was watching him. I stuck to my slower pace, waving to the Hernandez kids while they filled their inflatable pool with a big green garden hose, and smiling at Mrs. McCarthy, who was weeding her garden, as usual.

Hoot slowed down next to me and I pointed out the Coopers' place, where the meanest Doberman on earth lived, and the Wus' house, since they let me dig through the prickles to pick the juiciest blackberries from their bushes every summer. I told him how Mom froze whatever I came home with and made pies and crumbles for the winter holidays.

"So, you're going into sixth grade?" I asked as we turned toward the park.

"Yup. You too?"

"Yeah. I'll take you by the school so you can see where it is. There's a bus that comes down our street, but when the weather's good I usually ride my bike. It's not that far."

"Cool," Hoot said.

"I'll show you the library, too."

"Is there a skate park around here?"

"Kind of. There's a place where the older boys go. It's not like an *official* skate park, but lots of kids hang out there."

"We had a huge one near our house in Philly and my buddies and I used to go there every day, trying out new tricks and stuff." His voice sounded kind of sad.

"Why did you move here?"

Hoot frowned, stopped pedaling, and just coasted. "Because of my dad's job."

"Oh."

"It's crazy, because he won't even be around. He spends the week traveling and only comes home on the weekends." He shook his head. "We should have just stayed where we were."

I was stunned. "You only see your dad two days a week?"

"It stinks," Hoot said with a shrug. "But it's not like he's into the whole father-son thing anyway."

"What do you mean?"

"I don't know." He shrugged again. "I guess he didn't want kids as much as my mom did or something."

I didn't know what to say. I'd never heard of a father like that. Sure, some of the kids at school had divorced parents and only saw their dads part-time, but usually the dads were happy to see them and tried to make up for lost time by doing fun stuff, like seeing a movie or going bowling.

I'd never heard of a dad who wasn't "into" being one.

"Do you have brothers and sisters?" I asked.

"Two older brothers. James is in college already and Matthew's starting this fall at State. It's just me and Mom at home."

I thought about the craziness at my house. There was always someone around (too many someones, in fact). I couldn't imagine how strange it would feel to be a family of two.

"My mom rocks, though," Hoot added. "She's like two parents in one anyway."

"Oh," I said, but I wasn't sure whether he truly believed it, or if he just wanted to.

We stopped talking for a little bit and just rode.

I couldn't stop thinking about how sad I'd be if Dad and I didn't have our morning swim sessions, or if he wasn't there to tuck me in at night.

I watched Hoot ride ahead for some more jumps and wondered how much it really bothered him.

"Hey," I called to him, "Grandma gave me some money for us to get ice cream later on."

"Cool!"

I wasn't dumb enough to think a scoop of chocolate was as good as time with his dad, but I couldn't think of anything else to say.

There were a bunch of kids in Cedar Bow Park, so I kept on pedaling, hoping Hoot wouldn't want to stop there.

"Hi, Callie," nosy Beth Oberman shouted from the swings.

"Hi," I called back, with a quick wave.

The last thing I needed was Beth poking around in my business. I could still see her eyes shining with excitement the moment she told me Amy wasn't my friend anymore.

She may not have been a liar, but she was still a jerk.

"Come here!" she shouted.

As much as I wanted to keep going, there was no point in trying to outrun her. She'd just hunt me down like a bloodhound trained to track gossip anyway.

I hit the brakes, and so did Hoot.

"Who's she?" he asked.

"You'll see," I groaned. "Just let me do the talking."

Hoot laughed quietly, but only because he didn't know any better. They probably didn't make girls like Beth Oberman in Philly.

We pushed our bikes to the wooden fence that surrounded the park and waited for her to walk over. She was sucking on a lollipop and I must confess I really wanted her to choke on it. Not die or anything. Just lose the power of speech long enough for us to escape.

"Hi, Callie," she said, but she was looking at Hoot.

"Hi," I muttered.

She glanced at me, then back at Hoot, then me again. "So?"

"So what?" I asked.

She frowned, then turned back to my new friend. "I'm Beth."

"I'm Hoot."

"Hoot?" she asked, making a face like the name tasted bad in her mouth.

"Yup."

"Why?"

"Why not?" He shrugged.

"No," Beth said, glaring. "I mean why Hoot?"

"And I," he said, leaning toward her with a big smile, "mean *why not?*"

Beth glared at me, like I had any control over him, but I just shrugged.

"Is he your *boyfriend*?" she sneered.

Before I could tell her he wasn't, Hoot said, "Well, I'm a boy, and I'm her friend, so I guess I . . ."

"No!" I gasped, desperate for him to stop right there. "He's just a friend."

"Oh, *really*?" Beth asked, smirking at how uncomfortable I was.

"Yes," I told her as firmly as I could. I pretended to check my watch. "Hey, we've got to get going, Hoot." I hopped on my bicycle and headed back toward the street.

"Where?" Hoot asked, following behind me.

"See you later, Beth!" I called over my shoulder, then took off like I was in the Tour de France.

Hoot caught up to me in less than ten seconds.

"What's your problem, Callie?" he asked.

"Nothing," I said, in between panting breaths.

"So, why the big hurry?"

I slowed down so I could say my piece. "Look, I don't need everybody talking about this."

"About what?" he asked.

"You know. *Us.*"

His brakes screeched and when I turned, he was at a complete stop.

I pedaled back to him.

"*Us?*" he asked, sounding as disgusted as Kenneth was when he had to change Clay's diaper.

"Yeah," I said. "I mean—"

"What, because I'm a guy and you're a girl?"

"Well, yeah."

He didn't speak right away, but when he did, he was very quiet and serious. "I don't want to be your boyfriend, Callie."

He didn't say it in a mean way, but I was still embarrassed.

Did he think that's what I wanted?

"I know," I told him, my face hot.

Why did I have to open my big mouth?

It always made things worse.

He sighed and wiped his forehead with the back of his hand, which made his helmet lean crookedly to one side. "I'm totally new here, Callie."

"I know," I said again, quietly.

"I moved all the way from Philly and I don't know anybody in this whole city."

"I know." I bit my lip, feeling like a creep.

"Man," he said, shaking his head. "You keep saying that, but the truth is, you don't know *anything*." He turned his bike around in the direction of home.

"Hoot," I called after him, anxious to fix the mess I'd made. "We're supposed to get ice cream."

"No, thanks." He started to ride away.

"Come on, I've got ten dollars to spend."

He turned and circled back toward me.

I was relieved, until I saw that he wasn't going to stop. Instead he pedaled around me slowly, and said, "We can't go for ice cream, Callie."

"Why not?"

"Because someone might see us there together."

"It doesn't matter," I lied.

My brain was filled with visions of Amy and Samantha sitting in the corner booth, whispering and pointing at me. I cringed at the thought, and he must have seen me do it.

"Yes," Hoot said, and it sounded almost like a hiss. "It matters to you." He rode away again.

"Hoot!" I shouted after him, but he didn't stop.

He didn't even turn around.

I stood there, waiting for him to change his mind and come back, but he didn't.

Just before he turned the corner onto Third Street, he called over his shoulder, "All I wanted was a friend, Callie," and disappeared.

The worst part was, a friend was all I wanted, too.

Chapter Six

I didn't see Hoot for a couple of days. In fact, I didn't see much of anything but the inside of my house, since Mom really did ground me.

When he heard about it, Kenneth laughed and showed me the definition of the word *ironic* in the dictionary.

It was a perfect fit.

Mom said that even though I'd done a great job cleaning the kitchen and living room, and gone beyond what she expected me to do, she still felt that I needed to learn a lesson.

It seemed to me that shame and embarrassment over the pool incident was like a couple of lessons rolled up in one tight package, but I guess that wasn't the case.

As I gradually crossed items off of Mom's endless "to do" list in the mornings, I watched out the window for Hoot, but never saw him in his yard or out in the street.

It didn't take very long to be bored out of my mind, but luckily Uncle Danny got a job at the car wash on Madison and started leaving in the mornings at the same time as Mom and Dad. That meant someone had to be in charge of feeding the ferrets while he was gone.

That someone was me.

"What are they for?" I asked him, while he was showing me what I needed to do.

"Well, I've got six males and six females, so I'm partnering them for breeding," he told me.

"Breeding?" I asked.

"As pets."

"Oh."

I couldn't think of a single person I knew who had a ferret, and if that was his big moneymaking idea, I felt sorry for him. Ferrets for pets? He should have been breeding those orange monkeys with the big lips or flat-faced Persian cats. Something people actually *wanted*.

That wasn't the only reason I felt sorry for Uncle Danny, though. He was staying with us because his wife, my auntie Donna, had kicked him out of their house, and I'd overheard Dad telling Mom that he thought it was about time his brother got his act together. Uncle Danny didn't talk about it, but I could tell he was unhappy.

He was a much younger brother, so Dad tried to watch out for him, the same way I watched out for Clayton. Lucky for Dad, Uncle Danny wasn't in the habit of trying to eat crayons, but Dad had his hands full anyway.

"Once this business takes off, I'm golden," Uncle Danny said, opening a new bag of food pellets.

"Sure," I said, doing my best to sound positive.

"They're extremely intelligent creatures, Callie. There's no limit to what they can do."

When it came to making a huge mess of their cages and stinking up the garage, he was right.

There was no limit.

I tried to ask my next question as nicely as I possibly could. "So, how long do you think you'll be staying with us?"

"Geez, I don't know. Until these guys start flying out the door as fast as I can raise them, I guess."

In that case, he'd probably be living with my parents longer than *I* would.

I liked the ferrets and everything. I mean, they had sweet faces and soft fur, but they didn't really *do* anything but sleep and squeak every now and then. Stinking seemed to be their full-time job.

Between taking care of them and walking Babs and Roger (whose little wiener-dog legs could only go so far), I only managed to use up about an hour of my grounded days.

I ended up spending a bunch of time with Grandma, who wasn't exactly *fun*.

If she wasn't watching *Oprah*, she was watching game shows, and in between were the goofy daytime dramas.

One morning, she flipped the channel to *Love's River*.

"Darn it all. Repeat!" She sighed and shook her head.

A repeat?

That was an open invitation to say good-bye to boredom!

"Do you want to play a card game?" I asked, picturing the two of us battling it out over Go Fish, like kids on TV always did with their grandparents.

"Nah," she said.

"What about drawing?" I had two sketchbooks and I was perfectly willing to sacrifice one.

"I don't think so," she said, reaching for her tea and taking a sip. To my surprise, she wasn't even changing the channel to look for something else.

Oh, fish sticks.

"You mean you're going to *watch* the repeat?" I asked her, disappointed.

"That's right."

"But you've already seen it." I knew I was whining, but I couldn't help it.

"I might have missed something the first time around," she said. "Something important."

Yeah, right. It was a freaking television show.

I got off the couch and wandered out to the garage to feed the ferrets.

While I was pouring pellets into the open cages, I heard a garage door rumbling.

Hoot!

I dropped the bag and ran into the driveway, hoping it was him.

When I got to the other side of the hedge, there he was, crouched on one knee, pumping air into his bike tire.

Suddenly, I felt shy and didn't know what to say, so I just said, "Hoot" quietly.

He looked up at me, and I saw him start to smile before he forced his lips into a frown, like he'd forgotten he hated me, but remembered again, just in time. "Hey," he muttered.

"Look," I said, digging around in the dark corners of my brain for the right words, "I'm really sorry about the other day. I'm grounded, so I couldn't come over and tell you in person, but—"

"But what?" he asked, resting one hand on his knee and giving me an impatient look.

"I'm just . . . look, I'm sorry, Hoot. I was a real jerk."

He stood up and wiped the dust from the knees of his jeans. "Yeah, you kind of were."

Okay, I deserved that.

"I really *would* like to be friends," I told him.

It was true.

He was quiet for a moment and I anxiously waited to hear what he had to say.

"So would I," he finally told me, then reached over his bike to shake my hand. "So, no more apologizing. We're officially friends."

"Officially," I agreed, liking the sound of it.

"So, you want to—" His eyes suddenly bugged open and I turned to see what he was staring at.

The ferrets were on the loose!

I'd left the stupid cage door open.

I started to run.

Hoot was right beside me. "Rats?"

"Ferrets," I gasped.

"Ferrets?"

I had no time to explain, because three of the sneaky little guys were racing toward the backyard and more were slipping out of the cage.

"You catch those ones," I said, pointing toward the backyard. "I'll seal the cages."

"With Krazy Glue, I hope," Hoot said as he took off chasing them.

Luckily, it looked like only two more had escaped, and they'd both stopped to investigate the pile of food pellets that had dribbled out when I dropped the bag.

I tiptoed toward them, holding my breath, but they were so busy with the food they didn't notice me.

As quietly as I could, I closed the latch on the cage so the others wouldn't make a break for it.

I exhaled, took another deep breath, then reached for both creatures at the same time, afraid that if I only grabbed one, the other would run. Just as the one on the left turned to look at me, I pressed a hand down on each of their hunched backs, gently pinning them against the concrete.

The bigger one got ticked off right away and started squirming. It was like trying to hold on to a snake, the way he wriggled around, and the more he moved, the more the other one copied him.

I pushed their two bodies together and lifted them at the same time. I was pretty proud of myself until I realized that I couldn't hold on to both of them *and* open the cage.

I clutched the ferrets against my chest, whispering that everything would be okay, but that didn't calm them down at all.

I couldn't do anything but wait for Hoot, so I carried the critters to the backyard. He'd already caught all three of the escapees, but was stuck in the same position as me.

Neither of us had a free hand to open the cage.

We stared at each other for a minute, and as much as I wanted to laugh at the stupid situation we were in, I knew that losing even one of the ferrets would upset Uncle Danny.

"Is your grandma home?" Hoot asked.

Grandma?

"Yeah, but—"

"If she could just help us out for a second—"

"I don't think so," I told him, shaking my head.

"But she could—"

"Have another stroke or something. She *hates* them."

He tilted his head to get his hair out of his eyes. "Callie, we can't do it without her."

I thought about my screaming grandmother for a full ten seconds, the ferrets squirming for every one of them.

"Fine," I finally said, walking toward the front door. "I guess you're right."

"Callie?" Hoot said from behind me.

"Yeah?" I turned to face him.

"I'm usually right." He laughed. "You'll just have to get used to it."

"Very funny," I said, leading the way.

When I reached the door, I had to twist myself like a pretzel to hit the bell with my elbow.

Six times.

"Soap opera," I explained, when she didn't answer right away.

"*Love's River?*" Hoot asked.

My jaw dropped. "How did you know?"

"My brother's girlfriend used to watch it all the time."

"Ugh."

"Double ugh," he groaned.

At that very second, Grandma opened the door so fast I didn't have time to warn her.

She let out a scream that could have been heard underwater.

In Tokyo.

"Grandma, it's okay!" I shouted, trying as hard as I could to keep my grip on the ferrets, who were freaking out and digging their pointy claws into my arms.

I could hear Babs and Roger going crazy, barking their heads off inside.

With my luck, Babs would pee on the carpet in all the excitement and I'd be stuck cleaning up the mess.

Grandma kept screaming and grabbing at the hem of her nightgown, as if the ferrets wanted to get away from us just so they could run up her veiny legs.

"Grandma!" I yelped, hoping to snap her out of it.

"What's going on over there?" Mr. Owens, from next door, shouted. "What's all that racket?"

"Everything's fine!" I shouted back, over Grandma's screams.

"What are you doing?" he asked. He opened his gate and walked toward us.

"Nothing," I told him. The last thing I needed was for him to tell Mom that I'd been "playing" outside while I was grounded. Tattling seemed like just the sort of thing Mr. Owens might do. He was the one who gave Mom the full report when Kenneth accidentally broke Mrs. McGilver's basement window with a baseball, even though Mrs. McGilver had told Kenneth that if he paid for the repairs, she would keep it between the two of them.

"This isn't *nothing*," he said, then his voice boomed at Grandma, "Good grief, Dora! Enough of that screaming!"

She stopped instantly, and the neighborhood was dead quiet.

"Thank you," I whispered.

"You're welcome," he said. "Now, why are you terrorizing your grandmother with rats?"

"Ferrets," I sighed.

"Disgusting, filthy rodents," Grandma said.

"They aren't that bad," I told her, thinking about what Uncle Danny had said about them. "They're supposed to be very intelligent."

She leaned in for a closer look. "Hmm." She didn't sound totally convinced, but at least she wasn't screaming.

Grandma and Mr. Owens followed us into the garage.

"Good grief!" Mr. Owens said, when he saw the stacked cages. "How many have you got?"

"Twelve," I told him. "They're my uncle Danny's."

He put his hands on his hips. "Well, why aren't they at *his* house?"

"He lives with us."

"Is that right?" he asked, raising one eyebrow. "So it's your parents, three kids, your grandmother, your uncle, and twelve of these things living here?"

"And the dogs," Hoot added.

"Right," I told Mr. Owens. "Babs and Roger, too."

"Good grief," he said again.

He was beginning to sound like Charlie Brown.

Once we got the ferrets safely put away, Mr. Owens headed back to his side of the fence, muttering about "neighbor nonsense" while Grandma bent over to peer into the cages.

"Hmm," she said again, biting her lip uncertainly.

"So, you want to go for a ride?" Hoot asked.

"I'm grounded until tomorrow," I told him.

"Wanna go tomorrow morning, then?"

I did, but I had other plans. "I can't. I'm going to the pool with my dad."

"Oh," he said, looking disappointed. Then he brightened up. "Do you think I could maybe tag along?"

I almost said no, but stopped myself. Pool time had always been just me and Dad, and I liked it that way, but since I'd hurt Hoot's feelings and almost ruined our friendship before it really got started, I didn't want to blow it again.

"Sure," I told him. After all, there was plenty of room for three of us among all the old people.

"Cool," he said, giving me a thumbs-up.

I told him when to come over in the morning and he went home with a "See ya tomorrow!"

I turned toward Grandma, who was still staring at the ferrets. Strangely enough, she didn't look scared at all.

"I can't imagine what your uncle is thinking with all these things."

"He's breeding them for—"

"I know the plan," she sighed. "I just can't imagine what he's thinking."

"It might work out," I said, trying to sound positive, even though I thought Uncle Danny's idea was completely bonkers.

"Not a lot of meat on their bones," she said quietly.

Yuck!

"Well, I don't think anyone's going to eat them," I told her.

Although that might not have been a bad idea. Maybe Uncle Danny could sell them to local restaurants as fuzzy appetizers.

Grandma stood up straight and let out a creaky groan that sounded a lot like our basement door. "I meant that they probably don't stay very warm in the cold weather."

"Probably not," I said, lifting the pellet bag to finish feeding them.

"Probably not," she repeated, leaving the garage to finish watching *Love's River.*

What on earth was *she* thinking?

Chapter Seven

During dinner that night, I told Dad that Hoot wanted to go to the pool with us.

I ended up regretting opening my big mouth the second I'd done it.

All at once, like they'd been secretly practicing in the backyard for weeks, most of the table started oohing, ahhing, and making kissy faces at me.

Seriously?

Did they have to act like a bunch of second graders?

"So, when's the wedding?" Kenneth asked with a snort.

"Very funny," I said, popping one of the two brussels sprouts Mom said I *had* to eat into my mouth and chewing on the unholy green grossness of it.

"His name really is Hoot?" Uncle Danny asked. "I like it."

I only cared about what Dad thought.

"Do you mind if he comes with us?" I asked.

"Me?" he asked, reaching for the butter.

"Bill," Mom warned.

"Honestly, Carol, who eats broccoli without butter?" Dad asked, then looked to the rest of the table for support.

"I do," Grandma said matter-of-factly.

"Thanks for your input, Dora," Dad said.

"You're welcome." She nodded.

Even *I* knew he was being sarcastic.

I lifted the dish from the table and sliced off a chunk of butter for myself, which quickly melted on my steaming broccoli. When I looked at Dad, he winked at me, and I started to pass it to him.

"Your cholesterol is no laughing matter, Bill," Mom said, grabbing it from my hands. She put it next to Clay, who immediately stuck his hand in it and wiggled his fingers, digging deep.

"Way to kill my appetite, buddy," Kenneth muttered.

Dad sighed and sprinkled some Parmesan cheese on his green vegetables, as if that could camouflage the flavor.

"You don't mind Hoot coming, right, Dad?" I asked again, worried the request might have hurt his feelings.

"No, it's fine," he said. "I'd like to meet him."

"Don't you think Callie's a bit young for a boyfriend?" Kenneth asked.

"He's not my boyfriend," I snapped. "And don't you think you're a bit old for a teddy bear?"

Kenneth's eyes darted from Grandma to Uncle Danny. "It's not a teddy bear."

"Then what is it?" Uncle Danny asked. He held his fork, loaded with mashed potatoes, stuck in midair on the way to his mouth.

"It's . . . look, I don't have a teddy bear," Kenneth said, kicking me under the table.

"Ouch!" I reached down to rub my shin. "You're right, it's a stuffed *bunny*."

"Callie," Mom warned.

"No joke?" Uncle Danny laughed.

"He started it," I told Mom, for what might have been the twenty-six thousandth time in my life.

"And you can end it, honey."

The way she said it, I knew I was on thin ice.

Again.

"Fine," I said quietly.

"Fine!" Clay shouted, banging his fork on the table.

"Anyway, I think it's nice that you've made a new friend," Dad said.

"So do I," I told him. And despite all the harassment from my family, it was true.

When Dad and I left the house the next morning, Hoot was waiting for us on the front doorstep.

"You could have come inside," I told him.

"It's okay." He shrugged. "It's nice and quiet out here."

"You must be Hoot," Dad said, reaching to shake his hand.

"Yes, sir."

"Wow," Dad said, raising his eyebrows at me. "*Sir*? Kenneth could take a lesson or two from this guy, couldn't he, Cal?"

"Yup." I laughed, glad that Dad seemed to like him right off the bat.

On the drive to the pool Hoot asked what got me interested in diving.

"Him," I said, pointing at Dad. "He was the star of his college team."

"No way!" Hoot said, obviously impressed.

Dad shrugged, and I knew he was a little embarrassed.

"It's true," I said. "Tell Hoot about the state championships."

"It was a long time ago," Dad said.

"So was the Seventy-Sixers winning the NBA championship, but that doesn't mean it didn't happen," Hoot said.

"If you won't tell it, I will," I said. I loved the story. "Uncle Danny told me all about it."

"Oh, brother," Dad groaned.

"So," I began, excited to share the story, "my grandparents and Uncle Danny drove two hours to watch Dad compete at the state championships. When they sat in the stands, they saw all of these people holding banners that said stuff like 'I swoon for Boone' or 'Bring it home, Boone.'"

"Those were probably the only two signs for me in the whole arena," Dad said.

"That's not what I heard," I told him.

"I swoon for Boone?" Hoot asked, chuckling.

"Anyway," I continued, "Uncle Danny said they couldn't believe Dad had so many fans. I mean, they always knew he was good, but suddenly it seemed like everyone else knew, too."

"Diving was popular then," Dad explained. "Greg Louganis had won his two Olympic golds just a few years earlier."

"So, Uncle Danny said that Grandma started getting really nervous as they watched the other divers, twisting her ring on her finger around and around. My grandpa, who died before I was born, kept checking his watch, then the program, like, every thirty seconds. As each new diver went, even Uncle Danny started getting more and more nervous."

"Not as nervous as me," Dad said, laughing.

"So, when it was finally Dad's turn, he got out of the seat where he'd been waiting and walked toward the high board."

"You weren't wearing a Speedo, were you, Mr. Boone?"

"I was," Dad said, chuckling and resting one hand on his belly. "Like I said, it was a long time ago."

"So anyway," I continued, "Dad climbed the ladder and stood at the end of the board, and the crowd was totally silent."

"Probably stunned by my bathing suit," Dad said, laughing.

"And then Dad did something that no one had ever seen before."

"What?" Hoot asked.

"It didn't even have a name, so they ended up calling it a 'Boone' afterward."

"It was a combination of somersaults and twists that my coach had come up with," Dad said, always the humble one. "There were other guys on the team who could do it."

"But you were the first," I said.

"Yes," he admitted. "I was the first."

"Did you win?" Hoot asked.

"Yup," I said, as proud as ever. "He took home a big trophy."

"Where is it?" Hoot asked.

"In our garage, buried in a cardboard box with a bunch of old junk."

Dad looked surprised. "You saw it?"

I nodded. "I asked Mom about it after Uncle Danny told me the story."

I didn't mention that ever since the moment I held the trophy, I'd dreamed of winning one of my own. I didn't want diving just to be something Dad and I did together, I wanted it to run in our blood.

"His team won the state championships," I said.

"Did you go to nationals?" Hoot asked.

"No," Dad told him. "I injured my back, so I stopped competing."

"That stinks," Hoot sighed. "Well, did they win?"

"Nope," I said. "Not without Dad."

I grinned at my humble hero, waiting for the day I would be just like him.

When we arrived at the aquatic center, we split up to get changed, then met in the water, where Dad and I swam our usual laps of front crawl, then breaststroke, then backstroke, and finally butterfly, which was the hardest for me.

I would have rather skipped straight to diving, but Dad always said that it takes many parts to make a whole, and one of the parts that went into diving was building strength through swimming.

I had already learned that even on the mornings when it seemed impossible to drag myself out of my warm, cozy bed, once I got to the pool and felt my heart speed up with every stroke, it was always worth the effort.

Hoot wasn't much of a swimmer. He did a lap or two of front crawls, then used a kickboard to do a couple more. Soon enough, he moved to the kiddie pool, which was always toasty warm, and floated on his back, squirting water out of his mouth toward the ceiling, like a fountain.

In the big pool, other swimmers only used the outside lanes, so the middle was left clear for the diving boards. Dad and I climbed out of the water and headed for the shorter one, which I usually practiced on.

Before I could climb onto it, he stopped me. "So, what happened at the community pool?" he asked.

I stood quietly for a moment, just looking at him. He was big and strong, and even though Mom said his weight gain was a health hazard, I liked the fact that he was built like a hulking grizzly.

Thinking about the pool incident just made me want a bear hug from him.

I took a deep breath and told him about how the other girls talked me into diving off the big board, and what a disaster it had been.

"First of all," he said when I was done, "why did seeing Amy make you react that way? I know we haven't seen much of her this summer, but I figured she was away."

"She's around," I mumbled. "I guess."

"Callie, what's going on? I thought you were best friends."

Oh, fish sticks!

Why did we have to talk about Amy?

I didn't want to lie to Dad, because I'd always, always told him the truth (or at least the closest possible thing to it).

"So did I," I sighed and explained how she'd dropped me for Samantha just because I didn't like boys.

Dad looked confused. "What do you mean? You like Hoot, don't you?"

"No," I shook my head, a bit frustrated. Hadn't Dad been eleven once, too? "I mean *like*-like."

He scratched his forehead. "*Like*-like," he murmured.

"You know, more like a boyfriend," I told him.

His eyebrows shot upward. "You *like*-like Hoot?"

"*Nooo*." I smacked my forehead. "Maybe this is a Mom conversation," I suggested, even though she and I didn't really talk that much.

"Maybe you're right." He looked kind of relieved for a second. "But I do want to talk to you about the dive."

I raised one eyebrow. I'd been practicing in the mirror since I saw our neighbor do it.

"You mean the belly flop."

"Well, yes." He stared off into the distance for a moment, and I had no idea what he was looking for. Then I realized it was words. "You know, Callie, life is full of all kinds of people."

I thought about the melting pot. "Diversity," I told him. "We learned about it in school."

"Yes . . ." he said, then frowned. "Well, no. I'm talking about something else." He cleared his throat and looked at me. "Other people shouldn't dictate what you do, Callie."

"But I—"

"Just hear me out," he said, resting a hand on my shoulder. "You know what's right, Cal. You know in your gut when you're doing the wrong thing, and the older you get, the more attention you have to pay to that feeling."

"But they—"

"They aren't part of the equation, honey. You have to be responsible for yourself and not listen to what the other kids think is cool."

"I don't just do what everybody else says," I muttered.

"But you did the other day." He frowned again. "Let me ask you this. If no one had been there to see you do it, would you have climbed the high diving board?"

"I—"

"Really think about it before answering."

I did think about it, and the answer was a pretty loud "no" in my head. "I guess not," I sighed.

"I think that's a good question to ask yourself whenever you're facing a decision, Cal. Determine whether you're doing it for yourself, because *you* want to, or if you're trying to impress someone else who should really just like you for who you are." He winked at me. "And you know we're not just talking about diving anymore, right?"

I nodded. I knew he was right, but it wasn't going to be the easiest thing in the world to do. As far as the diving went, part of me still wanted to wow the other kids.

"I just wanted to show them I could do it," I said quietly.

He squeezed my shoulder. "You're not quite there yet, kiddo, but you will be."

"I hope so," I sighed.

He pulled me into the tight hug I'd been waiting for and whispered, "I know you'll make it. After all, you're Callie Boone."

When he let go, I smiled at him and climbed the ladder for the short diving board. I slowly walked to the end of it, counting off steps the way he'd taught me.

I saw Hoot watching from the kiddie pool as Dad guided me into the perfect position.

As I stood on the end of the board, I did all of the superstitious little things I always did, like tapping my bare toes against the grainy surface of the board five times, feeling the roughness, like sandpaper. I rolled my shoulders twice, then wiggled my fingers as if I was throwing away the nervousness.

I managed to block Hoot out of my mind while I carefully listened to Dad's instructions.

When he decided I was ready, I walked back to the ladder and took a deep breath. I didn't think of a single thing other than jumping as high as I could before arching my body for a clean entry into the water.

In my visualization, there wasn't even a splash.

When I made the dive a few seconds later, it felt almost perfect—a quick rush of air and the sensation of breaking through into a different world, with bubbles swirling around me.

I swam toward the surface with nothing but silence in my ears, and I didn't hear the whistling until I came up for a breath.

I looked at Dad, who was grinning and nodding.

I did it!

I could see in his eyes that he was proud of me, and I felt so good, I never wanted to leave the pool. I wanted to keep reliving that dive over and over.

I heard the whistling again and saw that it was coming from Hoot. I waved at him and smiled.

"That was awesome!" he shouted, and his voice echoed against the ceiling.

Dad and I kept working on the dive, and even some of the old people who'd seen me practicing before stopped swimming to watch and congratulate me on my progress.

I couldn't stop smiling.

When it was time to go, I quickly showered and changed into my street clothes before meeting Dad and Hoot in the lobby.

"I can't believe how good you are!" Hoot said, patting me on the back. "I don't know anyone our age who can dive like that."

"I'm still working on it," I said, secretly pleased.

Okay, not *that* secretly.

"She's been working hard," Dad said, pulling me against him in a hug.

"Hey!" Hoot interrupted. "Check this out." He had stopped in front of the bulletin board and was pointing at a yellow sign.

We took a closer look and discovered it was an invitation to try out for the Sunnyridge Seals dive team.

I didn't even know they had one!

"You should do it," Hoot said, nudging me with his elbow.

My heart started to race until I saw that the team was for ages thirteen and up.

"I'm not old enough."

"That doesn't mean anything," Hoot said. "If you're good, it won't matter."

I looked at my dad, who was carefully reading the sign.

"What do you think?" I asked.

He looked into my eyes, the overhead lights glinting off his glasses. "Is it something you'd like to do?" he asked.

I wondered if the Sunnyridge Seals wore matching swim caps and if they had a shiny team jacket. It might be nice to meet other kids who loved diving and swimming as much as I did.

I stared at the sign.

It was exactly what I daydreamed about, but never thought I'd be able to do until high school. I started to feel excited. The earlier I got going, the better my chances were of getting really, really good.

Olympics, here I come!

But I didn't say any of that.

I just nodded and said, "Yes."

Dad left me and Hoot at the bulletin board so he could talk to the lady at the front desk.

"Callie, you're seriously the best diver our age I've ever seen," Hoot told me.

I thought for a second. "But how many have you actually seen?"

He laughed. "Well, none, but man, it would be *so* cool if you made the team."

Excitement kept building inside me, and when Dad came back with a smile on his face, I practically screamed.

"With a parent's permission, younger kids can try out."

"Seriously?" I gasped.

"Seriously," he said, "but . . . unfortunately, you don't have mine."

I almost fell over.

"I don't?" I gasped.

Dad's expression was stern like Mom's until he started to chuckle. "You should see your face."

"But—"

"Relax," he said, patting my back. "I'm kidding, kiddo."

"So I can do it?" I asked.

"Of course you can."

"Awesome!" Hoot said, holding his hand up for a high five.

Dad and I each gave him one.

"You know, Callie," Dad said, "competing against older, more experienced kids won't be easy."

"I know."

"But it will be good practice for you."

I only had two weeks until the tryouts, so on the drive home, Dad planned our training schedule. We could go to the pool on our usual mornings, but also squeeze in some extra practices on Tuesday and Thursday evenings.

"You think I could watch?" Hoot asked.

"Sure, buddy," Dad told him. "You're part of this now."

"Cool," Hoot said.

I was so happy on the drive home that I didn't even think about what Mom would have to say about our master plan.

And that was a big mistake.

Chapter Eight

As it turned out, Mom had an awful lot to say at the dinner table that night, starting with an astonished *"What?"*

Dad explained, for the second time, that he had wrangled me the chance to try out for the dive team.

It seemed simple enough.

But it wasn't.

"Bill, she's eleven years old!"

"Almost twelve," I said quietly.

Mom didn't pay attention. "She could get hurt."

"She's not going to get hurt," Dad said, calmly spooning cauliflower onto his plate.

"How do you know?" Mom asked, quickly glancing at me, then back to Dad. Then she sort of stage-whispered, like I couldn't hear her, "I don't like the sound of this at all. She's going to be younger than everyone else, striving to keep up, and—"

"Honey," Dad said, gently shaking his head. "It's a tryout. If she's not good enough"—he gave me a wink—*"yet,* she won't make the team."

What?

It hadn't crossed my mind that I wouldn't make the team. All I'd thought about since the pool that morning was winning countless gorgeous, shining, flowing ribbons and doing commercials for Wheaties.

But what if I didn't make the team?

"I don't know, Bill," Mom said. "This is an awful lot to ask of a little girl."

"I'm the one who asked to do it," I told her, kind of offended by the "little girl" part.

"Oh, for crying out loud," Grandma interrupted, raising her hand to stop Mom from speaking, "they're not talking about jumping out of an airplane or—"

"Battling ninjas," Kenneth finished for her.

The table went completely silent.

"Ninjas?" Uncle Danny asked.

"What? I was just trying to make a point," Kenneth muttered, stabbing a piece of chicken with his fork.

"I think it would be cool," Uncle Danny said. "Like father, like daughter."

"Carol," Grandma said, looking into Mom's eyes, "just let her try."

I couldn't believe Grandma was rooting for me!

But that meant rooting against the drill sergeant, who never gave in.

Ever.

Mom shook her head and looked at Dad again, this time with disappointment. "I really wish you'd talked to me about this first, Bill."

"It's not that big a deal, honey."

"Yes, it *is*," I practically shouted. "It's a *huge* deal!"

"I know, Cal," Dad said, resting his hand on my arm. "That's not what I meant."

"I'd like to discuss this further in private," Mom said.

And that made me very nervous.

It took two whole days for Mom to approve the plan, and even though the wait drove me totally crazy, I forgave her for it as soon as I heard that she was going to let me try out.

I wrapped my arms around her, squeezing her in the tightest hug I could. "Thank you, thank you, thank you!" I whispered.

"Be careful out there, Callie. No crazy stunts," she said, kissing the top of my head. When we stopped hugging, she held my shoulders and looked into my eyes. "The only reason I didn't say yes right away is because I love you and I don't want you to get hurt."

"I won't," I told her. "Besides, I don't even know any crazy stunts."

She raised an eyebrow, but didn't say anything more.

I skipped into the living room, where Grandma and Kenneth were watching *Jeopardy*. Clay sat on the floor, staring at the screen and picking his nose in slow motion.

Gross.

"So, I'm trying out," I announced to the room.

"What is Mexico?" Grandma said, giving me a quick thumbs-up, her eyes glued to the screen.

The answer turned out to be Greece.

"Nice try, Grandma," Kenneth said. "And good luck, Cal."

I stared at him. It was the nicest thing he'd said to me in months.

"Thanks," I mumbled, completely shocked.

He shoveled a handful of sour-cream-and-onion chips into his mouth and crunched them loudly.

"Hmph." Grandma grabbed the remote to crank up the volume,

then picked up her knitting needles, which were the tiniest I'd ever seen.

That was strange, because she usually wrestled with thick ones while making the softest blankets in the universe. The needles she was holding looked more like toothpicks. Next to her was a tiny ball of fuzzy pink wool.

"What are you making?" I asked.

"A sweater," she said. "What is, oops, I mean *who* is Tom Cruise?"

The answer was Einstein.

"A sweater for who, Barbie?"

"No," she said, adjusting her glasses and continuing to knit.

"You don't want to know, Callie," Kenneth said, his eyes never leaving the screen.

"What is a train?" Grandma said.

The answer was a pogo stick.

Someone wasn't very good at *Jeopardy*.

"It's so tiny," I said, leaning in for a closer look at the perfect little square of pink that hung from the needle.

"You seriously don't want to know," Kenneth said.

"What is—" Grandma started to answer, but Clay cut her off.

"What ith poo!" Clayton said, and we all stopped to stare at him.

"Seriously?" Kenneth groaned.

"Number two!" Clay giggled, and by the time the youngest member of the Boone family pointed to his backside, we could already smell it.

"Code three," Kenneth said, plugging his nose.

"Code *four*," I told him. I had the feeling the change would require a silver suit and face mask from NASA.

"Mom!" Kenneth and I desperately shouted at the same time.

"I'm busy," she called back. She could probably hear the panic in our voices and knew exactly what was going on.

"Dad!" we called.

"He's in the garage," Mom called. "Busy."

Kenneth and I both turned to Grandma, hoping that the love of her youngest grandchild would be enough to push her into action.

Nope.

The only action she took was to pull a quarter out of her purse.

"You call it," she said to Kenneth.

"Heads," he said, crossing his fingers.

I crossed mine, too, and held my breath as she flipped her coin in the air. When it landed on the carpet, Kenneth and I both scrambled to take a look.

Tails!

"Yes!" I waved my arms in victory.

"Best of three," Kenneth said.

What a weasel!

Grandma sniffed the air, which was already pretty ripe. "There's no time for that," she said.

Kenneth groaned as he got off the couch and held out his hand for Clay to take.

My two brothers walked into the bathroom and I heard the fan start blowing. The room would probably be contaminated for at least a week.

Grandma and I were alone, and I found myself even more curious about her new knitting project.

"So?" I asked, poking the pink square with my fingertip.

"I'm making sweaters for the little guys outside."

I couldn't help picturing her squeezing them onto Mr. Owens's garden gnomes.

I was so preoccupied with the thought, it took me a minute to realize that by "outside" she meant the garage.

"You mean you're making *ferret sweaters*?"

"Yes," she said, sounding kind of impatient, as though it was the most obvious and natural thing in the world. She pulled the pink square so the ends met, making a cylinder.

"What about sleeves?" I asked.

She shrugged. "Their arms are too small."

In other words, she wasn't making sweaters, but wool tube tops.

How on earth were they going to stay on?

I didn't ask, mainly because I was scared she would answer.

When I told Hoot about it later, he flat out didn't believe me. As we pedaled to Sweet Dreams, the ten dollars from Grandma still burning a hole in my pocket, I kept telling him it was no joke, but he just shook his head.

"You know, if those ferrets are as smart as your uncle says, we should train them to do something," he said.

"Like clean up their own mess?" I asked. I'd had more than enough of that.

"No, like circus tricks. We could set up a show and charge admission."

"Well, it seems like Grandma has the costumes under control."

He laughed. "The Flying Ferretini Brothers!"

"Hoot, I think you might be nuts," I told him.

"Callie, I think you might be, too." He laughed again. "That's why I like you."

At that exact moment, Amy Higgins and her mother walked out the front door of Hair Today.

Oh, fish sticks and tartar.

"Callie Boone!" Mrs. Higgins said, with a big, red-lipsticked smile.

I hit the brakes, and Hoot did the same.

"Hi," I said, only glancing at Amy for a second.

In that second, I saw that her long blond hair had been permed and she smelled like chemicals.

"I haven't seen you for ages," Mrs. Higgins said, giving me a quick hug.

"I've been . . . busy," I told her, doing my best to smile.

And your daughter's a creep.

"Who are *you*?" Amy asked Hoot. She didn't even pretend to be friendly.

"Hoot," he said, nodding.

Amy made a face. "What kind of a name is *Hoot*?"

"It's a nickname," he said, but didn't explain any further.

He'd never even explained it to *me*.

Amy didn't bother to introduce herself.

"What's been keeping you so busy this summer?" Mrs. Higgins asked me.

I was trying to come up with something to say, but Hoot answered for me.

It was exactly what I *didn't* want him to do.

"Callie's trying out for the Sunnyridge Seals," he said. "She's been practicing her dives and—"

"Diving?" Amy snorted with laughter.

Her mother looked confused, just like mine had when Amy and I didn't speak the last time we were at Sweet Dreams. It was awkward, like Mrs. Higgins had no idea there was a big hunk of black pepper in her teeth and I couldn't find a nice way to tell her without embarrassing her.

She just kept smiling.

"Amy?" she asked, but my ex-best friend didn't say another word.

I knew she was picturing my belly flop and loving every second of it.

"Well, I think trying out for the Seals is a wonderful idea, Callie," Mrs. Higgins said. Then she turned to Amy and asked, "Is that something you'd like to do, too, honey?"

What?

Amy shook her head. "No."

"What about going to watch the tryouts and cheering Callie on?" her mother suggested, then turned to me. "When are they?"

The conversation was starting to make me feel dizzy and part of me hoped I would faint or something, just so it would end.

"The Saturday after next," Hoot said.

I couldn't help gasping.

"But I think they're closed to the public," Hoot hurriedly added, glancing at me with a worried look.

I gave him my most grateful (but shaky) smile. For that white lie, I'd gladly have a single cone and let him go for a triple.

"That's a shame," Mrs. Higgins said. "Well, keep practicing, and we'll see you on Saturday night."

"Saturday night?"

"At the sleepover," Mrs. Higgins said, with another confused smile.

Sleepover?

My stomach lurched.

"Saturday night," Mrs. Higgins said again.

I didn't know what to say.

I didn't know anything about the sleepover, and it was obvious Amy wanted it that way.

I couldn't believe she hadn't invited me!

For a few seconds, the faces of girls from school flashed through my mind, and I wondered if each of them was invited.

Did she invite Sara Cotter? Sandy Tran? Isabelle Hutchins?

Would they say rotten things about me, since I wasn't there?

I'd been to every sleepover at Amy's house since the beginning of time.

Even having Hoot next to me wasn't enough to stop me from feeling hollow again.

I stared at Mrs. Higgins, wishing I was better under pressure.

"She can't make it," Amy lied, giving me the kind of dirty look she usually saved for her older sister.

I didn't do anything!

I wanted to shout the words out loud.

The way Amy was acting, it was hard to believe she'd *ever* been my friend.

"I'm sorry to hear that," Mrs. Higgins said, and I felt so uncomfortable, I couldn't look at either of them.

When they finally said good-bye and left Hoot and me alone, he asked, "So, that was your *friend*?"

"Yeah," I sighed. "Amy."

"Hmm." He watched them turn the corner. "Kind of a turd."

To my total surprise, I snorted with laughter.

He was right. He had scabs on his knees, dirt under his fingernails, and a name that remained a mystery, but I doubted he would ever act like a turd.

As I watched my ex-best friend walk away, I couldn't decide whether I felt more angry or sad that she'd left me out.

I thought about all the birthday invitations I'd been given at school when other girls in my class watched and waited for the color-ful envelopes that never came.

I remembered how relieved I was at recess when Melanie Jackson handed me an invitation to the biggest tenth birthday party ever.

I remembered Danielle Newton crying when Melanie didn't invite her.

I'd seen it so many times before, but suddenly *I* was the one being left out, and it felt different.

I was the one on the outside.

I hated it.

"Ice cream?" Hoot asked, elbowing me.

"Yeah," I told him, leading the way. I thought about Amy's sleep-over and I forced a smile onto my face. I tried to convince myself that I didn't care who saw me with Hoot, or what they thought. In fact, once I parked and locked my bike, I marched into Sweet Dreams like I owned the place, wearing the biggest grin of the summer on my face.

I didn't fool anyone.

Chapter Nine

When Dad drove Hoot and me home from the aquatic center after a really good practice the next day, there was a strange white van parked in our driveway.

"What on earth?" Dad asked as he unbuckled his seat belt.

Hoot leaned as far forward as he could, peering out the window. "It says 'Animal Control' on the side."

We all got out of the car and Dad muttered something about Babs and Roger already having their tags.

Grandma was standing on the doorstep with a woman in a blue uniform, and from the hot pink color in both women's cheeks, to the hands on their hips, it didn't look like they were old friends (or new ones, for that matter).

"Thank goodness you're here," Grandma said when she spotted Dad. "This woman is giving me ten kinds of trouble."

"Sir," the woman said, tipping her hat to Dad. "I'm here in response to a couple of complaints."

"Complaints?" Dad asked, his eyebrows raised in surprise.

I was sure that, just like me, he was wondering who would complain about us.

Sure, the Boone family was weird, but we weren't a problem.

"One is a barking disturbance and—"

"Barking disturbance?" Grandma snapped. "Barking is what dogs do, and the two that live here do most of it inside the house. I know that for a fact, because they've driven me half crazy."

"More like three-quarters," I whispered to Hoot, who chuckled as he shushed me.

"Well, I realize that's what dogs do, ma'am, but this city has noise ordinances to protect the people who don't want to hear them."

"This is ridiculous," Grandma said, rolling her eyes.

"Dora," Dad warned her. "Please let me handle this." He looked at the officer. "What was the other complaint?"

She looked at her notepad. "Someone reported exotic animals on the property."

It took me a minute to realize she meant the ferrets.

"Exotic?" I asked, holding back a giggle.

"We have no such thing," Grandma snapped.

"They're hardly exotic," I added.

The officer frowned at me, like it was serious business, and my heart sank. "Miss, I need to see that for myself."

"You can trust me," Grandma said, with a brisk nod that evidently worked much better on kids than it did on officers from Animal Control.

"It's not a matter of trust," the woman told her.

"Oh, for Pete's sake," Dad sighed. "Let's just get this taken care of."

The officer told Dad she needed to look inside the garage, so the whole group of us walked out there, Grandma insisting that there was nothing to see, and my stomach filling with butterflies as I wondered what was going to happen next.

"It's okay, Callie," Hoot whispered, nudging me with his elbow. Unfortunately, it wasn't.

Dad opened the door and the officer shook her head when she saw the stack of cages.

Sure, there were a lot of them, but I'd done my best to keep them clean for Uncle Danny, and they didn't even smell.

"How many have you got?" she asked.

"I'm not sure," Dad said, looking to me for the answer.

"Twelve," I told him.

The officer pulled out her clipboard, looking annoyed. "This isn't a ranch, sir."

Actually, it was. A 1960s split-level ranch. But I had a sneaking suspicion that pointing out that fact wouldn't be appreciated, so I kept quiet.

"I understand," Dad said. "My brother is—"

"Are they licensed?" she asked, before he could continue.

"The ferrets?" Grandma asked.

"Yes, ma'am."

I couldn't help imagining them cruising around in tiny sports cars, even though I knew that wasn't what she meant.

Dad really looked like he wanted to say yes, but he sighed instead. "I don't know for sure, but I doubt it."

She moved toward the cages. "May I take a closer look?"

Grandma's fists were clenched at her sides in annoyance as Dad nodded, and the officer lifted one of the ferrets out of its cage.

She looked it over very carefully, from tip to tail, then put it back and lifted another out for the same inspection.

"I can see they're in good health. They're well fed, the fur and eyes look good—"

"See?" I said, hoping that meant the big inspection was over.

I was wrong.

"But the temperature is going to get too high in the coming weeks for them to be kept in here. Not only does this space lack air-conditioning but there's no fresh airflow."

"They get fresh air," I told her. "I open the garage door every day when I'm cleaning."

She leaned over to look me right in the eye. "Does this look like a happy life for these animals?"

I glanced at the cages and had to admit, "Not really, but once they have their babies—"

"You're breeding them?" she asked, straightening to face Dad.

"*I'm* not. It's my brother, Danny, he's—"

"A licensed breeder?"

"No, he's, uh—"

She wasn't listening as she moved to another cage and checked two more ferrets, then the next two, and the next.

To my surprise, she started to smile.

"What is it?" Grandma asked worriedly.

"These animals won't breed."

"They won't?" Hoot asked.

"No," she said, and I could tell she was trying not to laugh. "They're all males."

"What?" Grandma yelped.

So much for pink sweaters.

"But," the officer continued, "that's beside the point. I'm going to have to take the animals to our facility in—"

"Oh no, you're not!" Grandma shouted, moving to stand in front of the cages.

First she was terrified of them, then she hated them, and suddenly she was knitting tube tops and protecting them?

I could barely keep up.

"This is just like the show I saw on war protesters," Hoot whispered. "Except for the ferrets, I mean. And the fact that your grandma's . . . well . . . really old."

Dad tried to calm Grandma down as the officer opened the back of her van.

Unsure of what else to do, Hoot and I lifted a cage each, to help her.

Just then, Uncle Danny pulled into the driveway and barely even stopped the car before he jumped out, his eyes wide and frantic.

"What's going on here?"

"They're taking the ferrets," Hoot said, lifting another cage.

"No!" Uncle Danny gasped. "Put them down, you guys."

"But—" I began.

"Callie, just do it!" Uncle Danny shouted.

Hoot and I set our loads down on the driveway as he ran past us and into the garage.

Worried, I followed him.

"This is gonna be interesting," Hoot whispered, right behind me. "And embarrassing, I'm pretty sure."

"No doubt," he whispered. "Your uncle's kind of a spaz."

"I know," I sighed. Sometimes I thought Uncle Danny had as much to prove about being responsible as I did.

In the garage, we found complete chaos.

Grandma was blocking the remaining cages with her body while Dad begged her to "be reasonable." The officer grabbed a cage and Uncle Danny shouted, "What do you think you're doing?" at the top of his lungs.

The noise was enough to bring Kenneth out of his bedroom and into the garage, squinting in the daylight. When he saw what was going on, he shook his head and said, "Here we go again," before groaning and going back inside.

While I watched in a state of shock, Uncle Danny wrestled one of the cages away from the officer and set it on the ground. He unlocked the door, lifted the startled ferret out of it, and placed him on the pavement. He gave him a little pat on the butt, urging him toward the front yard.

"That can't be a good idea," Hoot whispered.

Of course it wasn't, but that didn't stop Uncle Danny from reaching for the next cage and shouting, "Run!" at the freed animal, who was just sitting there, like a city bus was going to stop by and give him a lift to the mall any minute.

"Run!" Uncle Danny shouted again.

This time, he got the point across.

The ferret scampered off into the hedges and I wondered how on earth he'd ever catch it again. It wasn't like the little guy would stroll back to captivity when the coast was clear, slip into his hand-knitted, fuzzy tube top, and settle down for a nice afternoon nap.

Grandma released two more ferrets and Dad demanded that she and Uncle Danny stop immediately.

The ferrets seemed to think he was talking to them and froze in their steps for a moment or two before running to join their buddies in the hedge.

Hoot and I unlatched our cages and started grabbing bodies to let loose.

"Good job, kids!" Uncle Danny shouted.

Dad turned to give us a warning look. "Oh no, you don't," he said, his jaw pulsing. He was sweating and his breathing was heavy.

Hoot and I put the ferrets back in their cages right away, and then neither of us moved a muscle.

Uncle Danny reached for another cage and the officer moved in front of him.

"Let's not take this nonsense any further, sir."

"Oh, for crying out loud," Grandma said, clutching a wiggling ferret in each hand. "You're not the police."

"Maybe not, but I can still write him a ticket," the officer said. "I'm going to take a wild guess that no one has a license for these animals."

Uncle Danny just stared at the ground.

Dad ran his fingers through his hair. He didn't look like his usual calm self *at all*.

"Look, I know there's been a misunderstanding here and—" Dad started to say, but the officer cut him off.

"And we're talking about a . . . substantial fine."

I looked at Hoot, who saw my confusion and whispered, "Big."

"Listen," Dad said, stepping toward her with an apologetic smile, ready to negotiate but still out of breath and red in the face.

"I'm sorry, but I'm through listening, Mr. Boone. Now if you'll all stand back and let me finish my job, I'd appreciate it."

The group of us were dead silent as we watched her gather the last of the ferrets from the hedge and load the rest of the cages into the van. All I could hear were the squeaks of the ferrets and Uncle Danny mumbling about his livelihood being taken away.

"Did he make any money off them yet?" Hoot whispered.

"Nope. Not a dime."

Once the van was loaded, the officer let Danny know he'd be receiving paperwork in the mail, then drove away.

"Jerk," Grandma snapped.

Dad sighed. "Dora, she was just doing her job."

"I'm talking about you," Grandma said.

"*I'm* a jerk?" Dad's eyes bulged.

"Well, you didn't do anything to stop her," Grandma said.

"That's right," Uncle Danny agreed.

"Hey," I heard myself say, stepping toward Grandma. "You can't call my dad a jerk."

"I can, and I did," she told me.

"Well, take it back!" I shouted, angry that she'd be so rude to the man who took her in when she was sick.

"Callie, that's enough," Dad said.

But it *wasn't* enough.

"She can't call you that, Dad. She—"

"I said enough!" Dad yelled.

He hadn't shouted at me like that since he caught me trying to mow the lawn barefoot. I was so stunned and upset, it took every ounce of strength I had not to burst into tears.

I ran into the house, afraid that I'd start blubbering, and heard Hoot following me.

"Go home," I said over my shoulder.

"No." He followed me up the stairs to my room, and when I tried to close the door before he could get inside, he stuck out his foot to block it.

I gave up and flopped on my bed, facedown. "Maybe he *is* a jerk," I said into my pillow.

"No, he isn't." I felt the end of the bed sink as Hoot sat on it.

I rolled onto my back, knowing it was pointless to try hiding the tears that had started dribbling down my cheeks.

"Callie, your dad's awesome," Hoot said quietly.

Of course he was. So why did he have to get so mad at me? "I know, but he just—"

"You can't talk to your grandma like that."

"Hoot, you heard what she said to my dad!"

Hoot shrugged. "They're grown-ups. They have their own rules, you know?"

"Yeah, but—"

"You can't be rude to her."

"But that was the first time I ever—"

He gave me a long look. "I've seen you roll your eyes at her before, Cal."

"I know, but—"

He shrugged again and shook his head. "It's disrespectful."

I was so embarrassed, I couldn't look at him. I never meant anything bad when I rolled my eyes at Grandma. I was just trying to vent my frustration. And all I'd tried to do in the garage was stick up for my dad!

I didn't feel like I'd done anything wrong, but there was Hoot, making me feel like a spoiled brat with no manners.

"Are you finished?" I asked, wishing he'd just go home and leave me alone.

He stared at me for a minute, then finally said, "I guess so," and walked out the door.

Chapter Ten

I stayed in my room for what felt like hours, waiting for Dad to come up and talk to me.

To my surprise and dismay, he never showed up.

But Mom did.

"Do you want to tell me what's going on?" she asked, sitting right where Hoot had been, at the foot of my bed.

"I don't know."

She cleared her throat. "You don't know what's going on, or you don't know if you want to tell me?"

I thought about it. "Both, I guess."

"Well, then, let me start." She took a breath. "Under no circumstances are you to talk to your grandmother the way I heard you did today."

"But—"

"There's no room for buts on this one, Callie. And you owe her an apology as soon as we're finished in here."

"Fine," I sighed.

Nobody was on my side anymore.

Didn't anyone care that I was just sticking up for Dad?

"And I hear you were helping to set those ferrets free."

"Yeah, but Uncle Danny told me to. Me and Hoot both."

She took another breath, this one even deeper. "Does it seem like Uncle Danny is making the best decisions lately?"

I didn't have to think about that one at all. "No."

"You have to learn to use your own good judgment, Callie."

I stared at her. "But I'm supposed to obey adults, and Uncle Danny is an adult, isn't he?"

That seemed to stop her in her tracks. She thought about it for a second or two before answering quietly, "Good point."

Great.

One point for Callie Boone, seventy-three thousand for the rest of the planet.

"Is Dad mad at me?" I asked, hoping with all my heart that he wasn't.

"Not mad," Mom said, "just disappointed."

My stomach sank. Disappointed was even worse.

"You haven't been acting like yourself lately, Callie, and your dad and I are both concerned."

"Concerned?" I asked. It was the same word they'd used when they sent Kenneth away to camp when he was thirteen and liked playing with matches.

She rested her hand on my leg. "Your father disagrees, but I think things started to change as soon as you met this Hoot character."

"What?"

What did Hoot have to do with it?

"I don't think he's the sort of boy you should be hanging out with."

I couldn't believe it! "That's crazy, Hoot's—"

She shook her head sadly. "A bad influence, from what I've seen."

"Mom!" I cried.

What was she talking about?

"Look, we've had . . ." She lifted her hand to count on her fingers. "The pool incident—"

"I didn't even know him then!"

"This situation today with the ferrets, then with Grandma—"

"It's not Hoot's fault. None of it. I swear."

"You two were releasing the ferrets, Callie." She bit her lip, then said, "I'm wondering if I should go speak to his mother."

"No!" I gasped.

"I don't think you should be spending time with him anymore."

This was turning into the worst day of my life!

Fast.

I had to think of something.

"What did Dad say about him?"

She frowned, and creases appeared on both sides of her mouth. "As I mentioned, we're disagreeing on this issue."

"Please talk to Dad about it, Mom. *Please* don't say I can't be friends with Hoot anymore!"

What would I do without him? We had fun together, he was smart, funny, and I trusted him completely.

Mom rubbed her forehead the way she did when the sink was full of dishes or there was a credit card bill in the mailbox.

"Look, all I know is that the summer was incredibly peaceful until that boy moved in."

"It was peaceful because I was by myself the whole stinking time!"

Hadn't she even noticed?

She raised her eyebrows. "Interesting that you should say that. I ran into Mrs. Higgins this afternoon."

"*Oh*, great."

"She said you were acting very strangely when she saw you yesterday." Mom frowned. "Like you were up to no good. She said you never come by their house anymore and Amy doesn't understand what's changed between the two of you."

I couldn't believe my ears. "But Amy's the one who changed!" I practically shouted.

"Lower your voice, young lady," Mom warned.

"Amy's the one who changed," I said more quietly. "Not that anybody cares."

"Not that anybody cares?" Mom closed her eyes, like I was giving her a migraine, when all I was trying to do was explain.

I waited for her to say more, dreading whatever was coming next.

"I know how close you and your dad are, Callie."

"Uh-huh," I nodded, confused. *Now* what was she talking about?

"And I'm glad you get along so well." She opened her eyes and stared into mine. "But sometimes I need you to let me in."

"What do you mean?" I bit my lip because she suddenly looked so sad.

"I mean . . ." She blinked quickly a few times and I was amazed to see tears in her eyes. ". . . that I'm not some ogre."

"I know." Of course I knew that!

"Do you?" she asked. Her eyelashes sparkled with moisture. "Look, I don't always get to do the fun stuff with you, Callie, because I'm busy with housework, school, and keeping your brothers in line."

I nodded, and she rested a hand on my shoulder.

"And to be honest, sometimes I'm a bit jealous of your swimming adventures with your father."

"You are?" I asked, genuinely shocked.

To my huge relief, she actually laughed. "Yes. You're two peas in a pod, and I have to admit that sometimes I'd like to be a pea, too."

"Maybe you can be a corn niblet," I said, so relieved she wasn't going to cry or yell at me that I started giggling. "Or a green bean."

"Very funny," she said, leaning in to give me a squeeze. "You know, it's not always easy being the mom around here. I've got to juggle everyone's needs, including you kids, your dad, Grandma, and even Uncle Danny."

"I guess it would be hard," I said, imagining trying to make everybody happy at once.

It wouldn't be hard.

It would be impossible.

When Mom made dinner, Kenneth whined about not being able to wear his baseball hat at the table, Grandma shook about a cup of salt onto whatever she was eating, then complained that Mom's cooking was too salty, and I did everything I possibly could to avoid eating brussels sprouts, broccoli, or cauliflower. Uncle Danny didn't phone to let Mom know if he wasn't going to be home, Dad kept trying to sneak butter or extra salad dressing, and little Clay threw enough food on the floor to keep Babs and Roger slobbering all over the tiles until midnight.

And that was just dinner.

Mom lowered her voice to a whisper. "You know, your grandma and I don't always get along. It's been that way since I was younger than you."

I'd never noticed.

"Why?" I asked.

Mom shrugged. "I don't know. We've just got different personalities, I guess. We never quite clicked."

"Seriously?"

"Seriously." Her smile was sad. "We're mother and daughter, but we've never really been friends."

"But that's crazy!"

"Hey." She laughed. "In case you haven't noticed, sometimes families are crazy."

I stared at her like she'd lost her mind. "Believe me, I've noticed."

I'd said it was crazy, but the truth was I'd never considered Mom my friend either.

"I'd like it to be different between us, Callie. You're my little girl, and I want us to be close."

"So do I."

"You know," she said, leaning in like she was telling me a secret, "I used to be a little girl, too."

"Yeah, but you were also a drill sergeant."

She closed her eyes and sighed. "I sure was."

"Why did you quit, Mom?"

She opened her eyes. "Because I wanted a family and I thought a school schedule would be a better fit."

"Do you miss it?" I asked.

"Sure, but that was a job, honey. You kids are my life. Sometimes you have to sacrifice some*thing* you love for some*one* you love."

I reached over to give her a hug.

"So," she said, taking a deep breath. "Let's talk about what's been going on this summer. I want to know about Amy, the full story on the pool, and I want you to fill me in on this Hoot character."

I took a deep breath of my own and started talking.

It seemed like I spoke for hours about the things that had been happening since school ended. And Mom listened. In fact, she made Kenneth give Clay his bath and asked Dad to make dinner, which he did (well, he heated up some frozen pizza), just so we could be together.

It was funny, but I couldn't remember the last time it was just the two of us, and I liked it. Mom really understood how upset I'd been about Amy dumping me, and she even did her best to make sense of the pool incident. By the time I got to Hoot and explained what he meant to me, she was actually relieved that such a good friend had ended up right next door.

I'd convinced her!

Then we finished up with a long, tight hug.

"Stop in and see Grandma on your way to dinner," Mom said as she left the room.

I found Grandma in front of the TV, and when I sat down next to her, she barely glanced at me.

"Grandma?"

"Mmm-hmm?"

"Can I talk to you for a second?"

"You're talking right now," she said, changing the channel.

She wasn't going to make it easy.

"Grandma," I said again.

"What is it?" she asked, eyes still glued to the TV.

"Can you please . . . look at me?"

She turned toward me and waited.

I cleared my throat. "I just wanted to say I'm sorry for shouting at you today."

She looked me in the eyes, long and hard, before speaking. "When I was a girl, we didn't talk to our elders that way."

"I know, and I'm—"

"You *don't* know," she said, shaking her head. "We wouldn't have dreamed of it."

"I'm sorry, Grandma," I said again. "I was trying to stick up for my dad and—"

"And I was angry he wasn't sticking up for those ferrets."

"But he's my dad and . . ." I thought about what Mom said and decided not to argue the point. "I shouldn't have yelled like that."

I was relieved to see Grandma's face relax a bit. "It's okay, Callie."

"I'm really sorry."

"It's okay," she said again, putting her arm around me. "We all have our moments."

I sighed. "I seem to have more of them than most people."

"You're a kid," she said, giving me a squeeze. "You've got a million more moments ahead of you."

For the first time I could remember, Grandma didn't move away from me. Until Mom called us for dinner, she sat with her arm around my shoulders, and we watched TV together.

It felt good.

Once we were at the table, I watched how much time Mom spent getting everybody organized with their pizza and was kind of annoyed to see that no one even said thank you.

It was like I'd never noticed her before, and suddenly she had a spotlight on her.

I chewed my burnt slice of Hawaiian and promised myself that

I'd try to help Mom around the house even more, and try talking to her when I was upset about things.

"So, how about those ferrets?" Kenneth asked Uncle Danny as I was clearing the table (without being asked).

"Well, they're gone," Uncle Danny answered, his face all gloomy.

"Can you get them back?" I asked. I didn't love cleaning the cages, but if it meant Uncle Danny would be happy, I could tough it out.

I just wanted everyone to be happy.

"Sure, if I paid the fines and stored them somewhere else."

And that's when it hit me.

Since Uncle Danny already had a set of male ferrets (by mistake), all we had to do was get them back and buy some females. Then he could make double what he planned on. And if he made that kind of money, he could pay Mom and Dad back the money he owed them, which would make them really happy. Then he could start saving up for his own place, which would make them even happier.

And if there was some way I could help make this happen, I could be the hero.

I thought of the pink piggy bank on my dresser. I was pretty sure I had more than a hundred dollars in there.

My life savings.

"How much are the fines?" I asked, knowing he'd already stopped in at the Animal Control office to check.

"Well, I'll have to buy twelve licenses at one hundred dollars each and there's one penalty because the ferrets aren't vaccinated and another because I had more than four in the home, so I'm looking at fifteen hundred dollars."

Never mind the piggy bank.

"Maybe we could raise the money," I suggested, still anxious to save the day.

A hero.

"With what," Kenneth sneered, "a lemonade stand?"

I was about to tell him to buzz off when I realized it wasn't a bad idea. The weather had been hot enough, that was for sure.

"Why not?" I asked.

Kenneth stared at me. "Because it's stupid."

"It was *your* idea," I reminded him.

"I was being sarcastic," he said, then gulped his milk.

"How unusual," I muttered.

It didn't matter what Kenneth thought anyway. The idea was already swimming around in my head. After all, if I wanted to be more mature and helpful, raising the money was a great way to show my family how much I cared.

I was going to get Uncle Danny's ferrets back.

And that was that.

Chapter Eleven

Lemonade?" Hoot asked, when I laid out the plan for him on the way to the pool the next morning.

"You heard her right," Dad said with a chuckle. "My girl, the entrepreneur."

I didn't know what the word meant, but I sure liked the sound of it. It was like something from a spy movie.

Something exotic.

More exotic than ferrets anyway.

"And we have to make fifteen hundred dollars?" Hoot asked.

"Yup," I told him, hoping that enthusiasm really was contagious.

"Let's see how many glasses you'll need to sell," Dad said, stopping for a red light. "Fifteen hundred dollars at twenty-five cents a glass—"

What?

"We're not charging a quarter, Dad!"

He laughed. "That was the going rate when I was a kid."

"Yeah, but that was in the olden days," I reminded him.

"Ouch!" he said, resting his hand over his heart in mock pain.

"Callie," Hoot interrupted, "even if we sell it for ten dollars a glass, we'd have to sell a hundred and fifty glasses to make the money."

"Geez, Hoot. Who's going to pay ten dollars a glass? That's ridiculous." (It was another of my favorite words, which I didn't get to use nearly often enough, so I said it again.) "Ridiculous."

"My point exactly," he said.

The conversation wasn't going quite the way I'd hoped.

"Look, I have to at least *try*, don't I?" I asked both of them. "I mean, isn't it worth a shot?"

"You must be nuts," Hoot said, shaking his head.

"But that's why you like me, right?" I reminded him, thankful that the crabby, crying episode in my room the day before hadn't ruined anything between us.

"Yup." He punched me lightly on the arm. "Okay, count me in."

"What do you think, Dad?" I asked.

"I can't say I miss the ferrets, but I know they meant something to Danny. I suppose it can't hurt to try."

Then, just like the hundred times he'd heard it before, Hoot asked, "How about an 'I know you'll make it. After all, you're Callie Boone'?"

"Fifteen hundred dollars in lemonade?" Dad laughed. "That might be pushing it."

That Friday, Hoot and I spent most of the afternoon getting our grocery supplies together so we could be up early and ready to go on Saturday.

I was.

Hoot wasn't.

I'd never really thought about it before, but in all the time I'd known him, Hoot had always come over to *my* house. He was the one to knock on the door or shout over the hedge. I realized that as much time as we'd spent together, I'd never actually been to his house.

For the first time ever, I rang Hoot's doorbell.

When his mom answered, I didn't know what to say.

She looked like a doll, with dark hair and perfect makeup. She was wearing a pink tracksuit that I seriously doubted was for exercising, and she smelled better than Clayton did after a bubble bath.

And that was saying something.

When she smiled, she had big dimples, and I liked her right away. "You must be Callie Boone."

I nodded, suddenly too shy to say anything.

"Jacob's asleep."

"Jacob?" I asked.

Who was Jacob?

She laughed. "Your buddy, Hoot. As usual, my little night owl was up until the wee hours."

So that explained the nickname! I was glad I found out without having to ask him. It made me feel one step ahead, for once.

"But we need to get our lemonade stand set up."

"Right," she said, saluting me and chuckling. "Operation Lemonade Stand."

She invited me inside, where I was surprised to see almost no furniture.

The cream-colored couch looked expensive, like it should be covered with plastic so no one spilled anything on it, and even though the cushions were plump and welcoming, they looked about as well-used as her tracksuit. The top of the coffee table was made up of hundreds of little pieces of tile. A mosaic, like we'd learned about in art class. I could tell it wasn't a table for stacking magazines or resting your feet on, that was for sure.

"We're waiting for the rest of our things to arrive," she said. "Hoot's dad can't seem to decide which stuff to keep, so who knows what will show up, or when."

"Where *is* Hoot's dad?" I couldn't help asking.

"This week is Boston, I think."

"Oh," I murmured. I couldn't imagine Mom not knowing for sure what city Dad was in.

"Anyway, I've got a little table and chairs back here you kids can use."

She called upstairs to Hoot and it only took a couple of minutes for him to come down, mostly because he didn't bother with a shower.

And yet, he still smelled like cinnamon.

In less than half an hour, we had our stand set up at the end of my driveway, complete with the plastic cups Mom got at Safeway and a huge jug of ice-cold lemonade.

What we didn't have . . . were customers.

Mr. Lee jogged past and waved, but didn't buy a drink. Mrs. Evans walked her poodle right up to the table, then told us she might be thirsty after they'd been on their walk.

Great.

"Maybe a dollar is too expensive," Hoot said.

I disagreed. After all, lots of people lined up to pay three or four dollars for a stinking cup of coffee. "Maybe we need to advertise."

I raced inside for markers and paper, then Hoot and I made a bunch of signs. He turned out to be much better at it than I was. He did all kinds of cool lettering and the results looked almost professional.

"You're good," I told him, holding one up to admire it.

"I'm kind of into drawing and stuff," he said with a shrug.

We stapled the signs to telephone poles all along the block. I even taped a little one to Clayton's T-shirt when he came outside to sit with us.

The signs said things like "Quench your thirst and save the animals" to get people's attention.

The attention they got was from Mr. Owens next door.

"What are you kids up to?" he asked, squinting at us through his glasses.

"Selling fresh lemonade," Hoot told him. "Just a dollar a glass."

"A dollar!" He nearly choked.

"It's excellent," I told him. "You won't regret it."

He frowned, but dug into his wallet and handed me a crisp twenty-dollar bill.

Hoot pointed to our empty money jar. "Uh, Callie?"

"I don't have any change yet," I told Mr. Owens.

"Maybe you'd like twenty glasses?" Hoot asked hopefully.

What a salesman!

"Bah," Mr. Owens said.

"Bah!" Clayton sang back at him.

He pulled his wallet from his pocket again and stuck his hand out for the twenty. After he tucked it inside, he handed me a single dollar bill.

"One lemonade!" I bellowed, like I was a waitress in a busy restaurant.

"One lemonade!" Hoot shouted back, pouring Mr. Owens a glass.

"Good grief, you'll make me deaf," he snapped.

I put our first dollar in the jar and Mr. Owens asked, "Is this some kind of a fund-raiser?"

"Yes," I told him, watching as he took a long sip. "We're getting my uncle Danny's ferrets back."

All of a sudden, Mr. Owens really *did* start to choke, and while I was frantically trying to remember the Heimlich maneuver in case I had to save his life, he sprayed me and Hoot with a mouthful of lemonade.

Gross!

After coughing and sputtering for a few seconds, he placed both hands on our table and leaned in really close.

Too close.

"You're getting the ferrets back?"

I cleared my throat. "Uh, yes."

"Guess again, little lady. Those nasty animals will never set foot in this neighborhood again."

I glanced at Hoot, who looked as surprised as I was.

"That's right," Mr. Owens said. "My buddy Gary down at Animal Control is always happy to help me out."

"You're the one who called?" I asked quietly.

He gave me a mean smile. "And I'll call again. If you don't watch out, I'll have those yappy dogs impounded next."

"You can't—" Hoot began.

"Watch me, kid." Mr. Owens backed away from the table, pointing at Hoot, then me. "Just watch me."

"Can you believe that?" Hoot asked once he was gone. "He was like something out of a cartoon."

"Yeah. Too bad we can't whack him with a frying pan." I could practically hear the gong sound effect.

"Well," Hoot said, shaking the jar that held our measly one-dollar bill, "at least he didn't take his money back."

I looked up and down the street and couldn't spot a single potential customer.

"I think we need to crank things up a bit," I said. "Let's see if Mom will help us move to the park. There's usually a game or two there on Saturdays."

And boy, was I right about that!

When we drove up, there were already three adult softball games being played and tons of people were Rollerblading, playing Frisbee, and tanning.

"Jackpot!" Hoot shouted as soon as he got a glimpse of the action.

We made a deal with Mom that we'd watch Clayton all day (I know, crazy!) if she would bring fresh supplies to us every hour.

It turned out we needed them.

We quickly learned that the vending machine near the public restroom was out of order, and from the moment we set up shop, business was booming.

Hoot did the pouring while I handled the cash and Clayton shook a sippy cup filled with lemonade and shouted, "Mmmm, jooth!" whenever he felt like it.

When Mom stopped by with a new batch, she saw how busy we'd been. "Nice job, you guys."

"I know! We'll get those ferrets back, for sure."

"Well," she said, frowning, "even if some of the fines get taken care of and the ferrets go to a good home—"

"Don't worry, Mom. We'll get them back."

She winced, and I could tell she didn't love the idea, but she was willing to support me anyway.

It made me feel good, like she really meant it when she said she wanted us to be closer.

Two trips later, she brought not only the lemonade but a couple dozen lemonade *Popsicles*.

They sold like . . . well, like Popsicles on a scorching-hot day, if you know what I mean.

On the next trip, she wiped the sweat from Hoot's forehead, smeared sunscreen all over our faces, and took Clayton home for a nap.

By the time the games were over and the sunbathers were packing up, several hours later, we were wiped out and ready to call it a day.

I held the stuffed jar up for Hoot to see, and when I set it on the floor of Mom's van, we gave each other a big, sticky high five.

"That was awesome!" Hoot said.

"I know!"

After counting our profits twice on my living room floor, stacking bills, and piling up change, we had a total of four hundred and three dollars.

"That's it?" I asked, disappointed.

That wouldn't even get *half* the ferrets back!

"That's four hundred and three glasses sold," Mom said.

"Four hundred and three dollars more than you two had this morning," Dad added. He patted me on the back. "I'm proud of you."

"It's not enough," I sighed.

"But it's almost a third," Hoot said hopefully.

"It's not enough," I repeated, feeling totally defeated.

We'd failed, plain and simple.

"Did you honestly think you'd make fifteen hundred dollars in a single day?" Dad asked.

"Well . . ." I kind of did.

"It's like diving, honey. It doesn't happen overnight. You've got to start working on patience."

"But—"

"Look, let's have a bite to eat and head to the pool for a practice."

After a long, hot day and a big fat failure, I didn't feel like going, and he must have seen it in my face.

"Tryouts are in one week, Callie," he said. "If you want to be ready—"

I don't know what came over me, but I felt overwhelmed by everything all at once. "Maybe I'll never be ready," I said, hating how whiny I sounded but not able to stop myself. I couldn't seem to do *anything* right.

"C'mon, Callie," Hoot said. "You want to do your best, don't you?"

"Yeah, but—"

"Then quit feeling sorry for yourself and go practice."

I saw Mom and Dad give each other a look and I knew they were impressed with Hoot.

They weren't even siding with their own kid!

"Fine," I snapped.

"Fine!" Clayton yelled from his bedroom.

Hoot stayed for dinner, a meal I usually would have been excited about, since Mom had made lasagna, but I couldn't find the energy to care.

"Did Callie tell you we found out who called the cops on you guys?" Hoot asked, midway through the meal.

"The cops?" Mom asked, turning to Kenneth, like he'd done something she needed to hear about.

"What?" he asked, meat sauce dribbling down his chin. "Mom, I have no idea what he's talking about."

"Not cops," I explained. "Animal Control."

"Who made the call, Callie?" Dad asked.

"Mr. Owens."

"Next door?" Dad asked, obviously surprised.

"That old guy?" Kenneth asked.

"Edward?" Grandma pressed her hand against her chest.

"*Edward?*" Kenneth, Hoot, and I turned to ask her at the same time.

"What?" Grandma asked, shrugging. "I'm allowed to date."

"*Date?*" I gasped, completely shocked. "You dated him?"

"Oh, relax," Grandma said, scooping a forkful of lasagna into her mouth. "It was only a few times, and I broke it off."

"He was a total creep," I told everyone at the table. "He called about the ferrets and he said that he'd go after Babs and Roger next. He said he has a friend at Animal Control."

"Can you believe it?" Dad asked my mom.

Uncle Danny walked in and asked what was going on, and when I explained that we'd tried to earn enough money to get his ferrets back, his face turned red.

When I passed the jar of money to him, he wouldn't take it.

"You kids keep it," he said, clearing his throat.

"But we did it for you," I told him.

"I didn't ask you to do that, Callie."

"I know, but—"

"I don't want it. They told me I'd have to come up with a better housing situation for them and, on top of buying the licenses for them, I'd also have to pay penalties for not having licenses in the first place. This plan just isn't going to fly."

"Maybe you should try birds," Kenneth muttered.

Mom shot him a look that stopped him cold.

Finally, Uncle Danny suggested we give the money to Dad, to pay back part of his loan.

Kenneth should have been thrilled, since this brought him four hundred and three dollars closer to straight teeth, but he got all snotty about it instead.

"Great, next year they'll be calling me Brace-Face, Metal-Mouth, and Tinsel-Teeth," he groaned, leaving the table to stomp into the kitchen.

"You're welcome!" I called after him, super annoyed that the whole fund-raising event had been a disaster.

So much for trying to help out around the house.

"So, are we heading for practice, or what?" Dad asked.

Against all odds, my mood improved at the aquatic center and I was secretly glad Dad and Hoot had pushed me to go. I let everything that was bothering me sink to the bottom of the pool and concentrated on making my body do all of the things it was supposed to. With each dive, I was feeling happier and stronger about the tryouts.

"I know you'll make it," Dad said, flashing me a thumbs-up after a particularly good twist. "After all, you're Callie Boone."

On the way home, I was feeling so excited about what might happen at tryouts that it made me take a good look at the way I'd acted like such a whiny kid at the dinner table and even before that.

Not cool.

I was almost twelve, and that was too old to be acting like a baby when things didn't go my way.

I still felt a bit jealous of Clayton sometimes because everyone fussed over him and all he ever had to do was scream or cry to get what he wanted, but lately I'd been feeling more jealous of Kenneth.

He was almost *driving*, for crying out loud, *and* he had a part-time job ready for him when school started. Mom and Dad were always talking about how much more responsible he'd become, compared to the way he used to be, and they seemed really happy about that.

I wanted them to think the same kinds of things about *me*. After all, I was more grown up than I used to be, too. I was tired of Mom calling me a "little girl" and of people looking at me like a kid. I had ideas of my own—good ones—and I had opinions about things I'd never really thought about before. I was able to do more, too, whether that meant diving or helping around the house.

After a couple of minutes of thinking about how I'd behaved and how I wished I'd taken the mature route instead, I did something I'd never done before. I waited until Dad and Hoot stopped talking about Greg Louganis's medals and apologized to them for my bad attitude.

"It's just that sometimes when things aren't going the way I want them to," I tried to explain, "I get frustrated, and then everything just gets worse."

"Everybody feels that way sometimes, kiddo," Dad said, reaching over to pat my head. "But things always get better in the end, don't they?"

"They do," Hoot agreed.

"Yeah, they do," I said with a smile. "They always do."

Chapter Twelve

Dad and I went to the pool every single day that week. Sometimes Hoot came along, and other times it was just the two of us, the way it used to be.

With every practice, I became more confident. Not to the point of thinking I was guaranteed a spot on the team or anything, but confident that I had good control over the dives. Confident that I knew what I was doing.

Counting down the days was almost like waiting for Christmas, and I loved it. Every morning, I rolled out of bed, excited that I was one day closer to tryouts. Sure, there were moments when I was so nervous I doubted I could go through with it, but when I felt that way, I stopped and took slow, deep breaths and pictured myself slicing the water like a knife until my breathing slowed down to normal.

On Friday night, we had a final practice, with Hoot along for the ride. Everything went as close to perfectly as it ever had, and I knew I was going to have trouble sleeping that night.

Counting days was one thing, but counting *hours* was another.

"What time are we going in the morning?" Hoot asked on the way home.

"You're coming?" I asked, surprised to hear it. "I thought your dad was going to be here this weekend."

"Plans changed," Hoot said, his voice sounding a bit sad.

"That stinks! You were so excited, and—"

"Stuff happens," Hoot said.

I turned around to check out his expression, but he was looking out the window. I'd never even seen his dad.

"We'll leave here at ten," Dad said, "to get Callie there with plenty of time to change and warm up a bit before they get started."

"I can't wait," I said.

"Me neither," Hoot added, sounding more like his usual self.

"Well," Dad said, "you've practiced hard and shown a lot of commitment. All you can do tomorrow is give it your best shot. The rest is out of your hands."

"I know you'll make the team," Hoot said. "You deserve it, Cal."

"I hope so," I said, smiling as the butterflies flew around in my stomach.

I took my twelve-thousandth deep, calming breath and crossed my fingers.

The next morning, the whole family cheered me on at breakfast. Grandma pinched my cheeks really hard, Uncle Danny punched my shoulder, Clayton drooled in my cereal, and Kenneth gave me a mumbled "good luck" before yawning and heading back to bed.

When Mom, Dad, and I walked out the door, Hoot was waiting for us on the top step.

"Ready?" he asked, following us into the van.

"I think so," I told him.

I sure hoped I was.

I was nervous enough about the tryouts, but when I thought about the fact that Mom had never seen me dive before, the handful of butterflies in my stomach suddenly felt like a whole army.

I wanted to impress Mom, to show her how much I'd learned and how my hard work had paid off. I wanted her to see that I'd "taken on a challenge," as she liked to say.

I wanted her to be proud.

While Mom drove, Dad pulled a package out of the glove compartment and handed it to me. It was wrapped in pink paper with purple and yellow stars all over it.

"What is it?" I asked.

"Open it and see," Dad told me with a smile.

I opened the card first. On the front was a funny cartoon of a giraffe in a bathing suit. Inside it said: "Callie, we've never been more proud. Good luck! Love, Mom and Dad."

"Thanks, you guys," I said as I started to tear open the package.

Under the wrapping paper was a plain white box, and I couldn't imagine what was inside. When I carefully opened it up, I found a bright red bathing cap, like they wore in the Olympics, and a blue bathing suit with red and white stripes down the sides.

Racing stripes.

"Wow!" I couldn't believe how cool it was.

"You like it?" Mom asked.

"Yeah!" I thought of the purple suit I'd been using all summer and even though I'd never considered wearing something else, the new one was so much better, so much more grown up, I couldn't wait to try it on.

"The cap is what the older kids will be wearing," Dad said, "and Mom and I both thought the suit looked . . . professional."

"It does," I said. "Thank you, thank you, thank you!"

"You're welcome, you're welcome, you're welcome," Mom said, laughing.

When we got to the aquatic center, Dad and I went to the registration desk to sign up.

"You understand the minimum age is thirteen," the woman behind the desk said, looking me up and down over her glasses.

"And I understand that with a parent's consent, she can proceed," Dad said, sounding like a lawyer on TV.

I signed my name, skipping the usual heart I drew to dot my *i*, suddenly seeing it as childish. The woman pointed me toward the change room, where I'd gone a hundred times before.

But this time, the whole aquatic center felt different.

I was used to being surrounded by ladies who were at least Grandma's age, in flowery bathing suits and bright pink lipstick. But that morning, the room was filled with teenage girls. For some reason, I'd assumed that the kids trying out would only be a year or two older than me, but some of the girls in there looked more like sixteen or seventeen.

Suddenly, I felt like a little kid who was in the wrong place, and I was pretty sure a flashy bathing suit wasn't going to be enough to change that.

"Are you trying out?" an older girl with long blond hair asked me. She had sparkling green eyes and a soft voice.

I nodded. "Mmm-hmm."

"How old are you?"

"Um . . . almost twelve."

She smiled at me and stuck out her hand. "I'm Jessica."

I shook her hand. "I'm Callie."

"Well, good luck, Callie."

"Thank you," I said, grateful she hadn't told me I needed to go home and grow up.

I slipped into a stall, feeling too self-conscious to take off my clothes in front of the older girls. Luckily, the bathing suit was almost a perfect fit, and that made me feel a bit better.

When I had my cap on, I tucked my stuff into a cubby, trying not to draw any attention to myself, and started toward the shower for a rinse.

I stood quietly under the hot water while the older girls chatted and laughed together, like they already knew one another.

Every now and then, one of the girls would look at me like I was some kind of an alien, but I did my best to ignore it.

It was good practice for the next time I saw Amy and Samantha.

Even though I knew Mom, Dad, and Hoot were in the stands, I felt very alone and the nervousness really started to kick in.

"Let's roll," one of the girls said, and they all started to walk out to the pool.

I tagged on to the end of the line and followed them, like the smallest, least-decorated float in a parade.

The stands were only about half full, but that was still *way* more people than I expected to be there. When I searched the rows for my supporters, I spotted them right in the middle.

Hoot gave me a huge grin and a wave I probably could have seen from six miles away. I smiled and wiggled my fingers in a tiny wave back, too nervous to do anything more.

The girls in front of me settled onto a wooden bench, so I did the same, my stomach doing bigger flips than the rest of my body was capable of.

On a second wooden bench were the boys, who looked like grown men. One even had *hair* on his chest!

What was I thinking?

How could I ever hope to compete with these people?

I'd never thought about who else would be trying out. I'd been too busy imagining myself wearing a team jacket and filling my bedroom with trophies.

All I wanted to do was run back to the change room, throw on my clothes, go home, and pretend none of it had ever happened.

Then I looked up in the stands and saw Dad.

He was staring right at me and miming deep breathing.

Was he crazy?

Couldn't he see all the big kids around me?

Couldn't he tell that this was a terrible idea?

I was more scared than I'd ever been.

My hands were sweaty and all I wanted was to be back at home.

At least I wouldn't be humiliated there.

I tried to give him the kind of look someone dangling from a ledge or surrounded by starving tigers might give.

A "save me" look.

Instead of saving me, he gave me a thumbs-up.

I stared at him as he continued to demonstrate deep breathing, and without even realizing it, I slowly started to do it myself.

Inhale, count to three, exhale.

I closed my eyes as I breathed and imagined my feet taking slow, sure steps to the end of the board. In my mind, I heard the gentle squeak of the springs, felt the cool air against my skin, and smelled the familiar chlorine.

When I opened my eyes, Dad was still watching me, and smiling.

My panic was gone and I felt nice and calm.

"Thank you," I mouthed to him.

He mouthed back words I couldn't make out completely, but I knew from years of experience exactly what they were.

I know you'll make it. After all, you're Callie Boone.

I gave him my own thumbs-up, then watched as the coaches came out of the office in matching Seals tracksuits and found their seats at a big wooden table.

They didn't do much talking, but briefly thanked us all for coming out, then wished us good luck.

And just like that, they got started.

One by one, each of the big kids heard their name called, stood up, climbed the diving board, and, when they were ready, dove.

I couldn't believe how good they were!

One of the guys did a double somersault, and another aced a backward flip. A girl even did the most amazing twist, then entered the water without a splash. Some of the simpler dives were ones I'd tried myself, and others I'd only heard about from Dad.

Every now and then, I looked up at the stands, and one or all of my supporters would wave or smile.

Another diver took his turn, and another one after that. I watched it all, waiting for my own name.

Finally, I heard it over the loudspeaker.

"Callie Boone."

I stood up quickly enough that my breakfast shot upward in my stomach.

Please don't let me puke!

I stood still for a second, my hand resting on my stomach to make sure the eggs and toast were staying where they belonged.

When it was safe, I started walking.

I had to go past both benches of teenagers, and while the girls were minding their own business (aside from Jessica, who whispered another "good luck" as I walked by), the boys acted more like . . . boys.

It started with a snicker from a red-haired guy at the end of the bench, then the one next to him made some joke about me being in kindergarten.

Har-dee-har-har.

I kept walking and didn't look at any of them.

A handful of the boys teased me, so I pretended they were all Kenneth, which made it much easier to ignore them.

I heard one of the coaches say, "Only eleven years old," when I walked past their table, and felt my whole body get tense as I waited for them to call after me, telling me to go home.

But they didn't.

I kept going, stealing a quick glance into the stands, where Hoot's hands were in the air, fingers crossed on both.

I took another deep breath as I reached the bottom of the high board's ladder, then gripped the rails to start climbing.

With each step, I pictured myself hitting the water in a smooth motion. I imagined that it was an early morning practice. I could almost hear Dad telling me to pace myself on the way up and take the time to clear my head, the way he had for weeks.

He had prepared me.

For the high diving board.

Somehow, through pure concentration, my breathing was even and my knees were barely shaking when I reached the top.

The water looked cool and pure, and with no one in the pool, I couldn't see even the tiniest ripple.

It was perfect.

I took another breath, and then one last look at the crowd. I saw

Dad, Mom, and Hoot, all watching me, and knew that there was no one I'd rather have cheering me on.

But just as I was feeling ready to get out there and do it, I saw them.

Amy Higgins and Samantha McAllister were leaning against the stands, staring at me.

Oh, fish sticks, tartar, and a side of fries!

I gulped, and that threw my breathing off.

What on earth were they doing there?

Didn't they have better things to do than give me a hard time? Apparently not.

I quickly looked back at Dad, feeling anxious.

He couldn't see the girls, but the expression on his face told me that he knew something had thrown me off. He mimed deep breathing again and I slowly started to inhale, then exhale, doing my best to push Amy and Samantha from my mind.

"When you're ready, Miss Boone," one of the coaches said, over the loudspeaker.

That snapped me out of it.

I thought about how much this dive meant to me, and how little it mattered what those girls thought. They hadn't spent the summer helping me get ready, like Dad, or cheering me on, like Hoot.

The dive was for me and the people who truly cared about me.

No one else mattered.

I took another breath and slowly walked to the end of the board, feeling more confident with every step.

I counted to three in my head, the way Dad had taught me, and jumped straight up, then bounced once on the board before I was in the air.

Everything felt just right. My arms and legs were strong and sure, my back arched, just like it was supposed to.

It felt . . . awesome.

When I twisted into my finishing position, I entered the water cleanly and knew in my heart that it was one of my best dives ever.

I did it!

I wanted to scream with excitement underwater, but instead I blew bubbles of glee out of my nose until I reached the surface.

When I came up for air, there was no roaring crowd, but Mom, Dad, and Hoot were all standing up, waving their fists in the air like I was a champion.

I felt like one.

I swam over to the edge of the pool and climbed out, awfully pleased that when I walked past the bench lined with boys, they didn't say a peep.

I wrapped my towel around my waist and waited for my next turn. We were supposed to do three dives each, so Dad had prepared me. Mine were all pretty simple, because he said it was better to be good at something easier than bad at something difficult.

The other divers took their turns and each one seemed to get a bit more complicated than the last.

My second dive wasn't as good as my first, but it was what Dad would have called "solid." My third was better, but not quite perfect.

Overall, I felt good about the job I'd done, and since I was finished trying out, I started to get excited about the announcements of who had made the team. I could already see my Seals jacket hanging in my closet, with my name embroidered on the back in curly letters.

The coaches didn't make a big speech before they started naming new team members, but they told us there were only twenty spots to fill. Then they started calling out names.

Girls jumped off the bench with shrieks and giggles when their names were called, while the boys just nodded or patted each other on the back.

It didn't take much time at all before they were down to the last two spots. I was still feeling positive, but nervousness was taking over, too.

"Brian Packer," the female coach said, and a dark-haired boy smiled.

One spot left.

What if I didn't make it?

At that moment, I couldn't imagine anything worse. Nothing on earth would be more disappointing than . . .

I *didn't want to think about it.*

"Audrey Kwan," the coach said.

The girl next to me gasped, "That's me!"

My heart sank. Not just a quick dip into my stomach, but a plunge down to my ankles. I'd worked *so* hard, and they didn't want me. I could feel tears starting, but didn't want to cry like a kid in front of everyone, so I dug my fingernails into the palms of my hands as a distraction while the coaches thanked everyone for coming.

I couldn't even look at the stands.

As I stood up to leave with the rest of the kids, the female coach's voice came over the loudspeaker.

"For those of you who didn't make it this time, please come back and try again in January. There were some excellent divers here today, but we simply don't have room for everyone."

I got dressed in a stall in the locker room, wishing I was one of the girls I could hear everyone congratulating.

A couple of tears ran down my cheeks, but I wiped them away with my sleeve before leaving the stall. I slipped my bag over my shoulder and walked toward the door.

"Great job, Callie," Jessica said with a smile. "I was really impressed."

"I didn't make it," I said, even though she already knew that.

"Hey," she said, her smile widening, "neither did I. That was my third try, but we'll just have to try again, right?"

"Sure," I said, but I wasn't sure at all.

Her third try?

The truth was, I'd done my very best, and it just wasn't good enough.

I waved good-bye to Jessica, grateful that she'd been so nice and friendly toward me, and walked out to the lobby.

Mom, Dad, and Hoot were there waiting for me, smiling and excited, as though I'd made the team.

"Oh, honey," Mom said, pulling me into a tight hug. "I'm so proud of you!"

"But I didn't make it," I told her.

Weren't they listening to the announcements?

Dad hugged me next. "Cal, that was absolutely the best job I've ever seen you do on a forward dive. Just fantastic."

When he let go of me, Hoot gave me a high five. "Man, you were awesome!"

"But I didn't make the team," I said again, totally confused.

"But the important thing is, you tried," Mom said. "And you'll try again next season."

"You're at least two years younger than everybody out there, and you gave them a run for the money," Dad said, patting my back. "Not only that, but you achieved your personal best. That's really something to be proud of."

I thought about it on the way out to the car, while the three of them were talking.

It really was my personal best, and it had felt so good to try. I still desperately wanted to have made the team and to have my own jacket. I was still disappointed and heartbroken, but I also had to consider that maybe I was just . . . a little early.

When I buckled my seat belt, I asked Dad, "So, you really think I should try out again in January?"

"Of course," he said with a laugh. His eyes met mine in the rearview mirror. "I know you'll make it—"

Mom and Hoot joined him for the rest, as they all shouted, "After all, you're Callie Boone!"

Chapter Thirteen

In the following days, I was too disappointed to even think about trying out next time. It was so hard to go through all of that practice, all of that training, and to do my best, only to fail. I didn't like to think about letting my family down and I wasn't sure I could handle trying out again.

Dad reminded me that I had months to decide. In the meantime, we still hit the pool, partly because it couldn't hurt to be prepared, but mostly because neither of us wanted to stop.

Soon enough, there were only three more weeks of summer left to enjoy, which was almost impossible to believe.

Hoot and I hung out together almost every day. If we weren't riding bikes, we were drawing at the picnic table in my backyard or playing soccer in the park with whoever happened to be around.

It was fun to introduce him as my friend, and it felt good to know that when school started, Hoot and I were in it together. We already knew from the school mailer that we'd be in the same sixth-grade class, and we were both happy about that.

Especially me.

When we were bored one afternoon, we offered to throw another lemonade fund-raiser for Uncle Danny, but he didn't seem to have any interest at all. In fact, he barely spent any time at the house anymore. He just came home from work, showered, shaved, and then left again, smelling like about a hundred acres of evergreen forest.

"Where does he go?" Hoot asked, when we were lying on the grass in the backyard and staring at the sky after lunch one day.

"I don't know," I told him.

"When does he come home?"

"After I'm asleep."

"Hmm." Hoot scratched his head. "Maybe he's a CIA operative."

"Uncle Danny?" I laughed. "Yeah, right."

"Okay, maybe not." Hoot thought some more. "What if he's an undercover cop?"

"Ha! Can you be serious?"

"Okay, okay. Maybe he has a second job or something. Like a taxi driver."

"Or a baker." Somehow the idea of Uncle Danny elbow deep in muffin batter didn't seem too likely.

"Maybe he has a girlfriend," Hoot said with a shrug.

"I don't know. I kind of doubt it. He said he was finished with women when Auntie Donna kicked him out."

"It's a mystery," Hoot sighed.

"Yup. Too bad you aren't Nancy Drew."

"We should tail him some night."

I laughed. "Have you been staying up watching police shows or something?"

He laughed, too. "There were a bunch of old cop movies on Channel Four this week, and when I can't sleep—"

"You hoot with the owls," I said, smiling to myself.

That caught him off guard. "Hey, how'd you know that?"

"Your mom told me ages ago. Why can't you sleep anyway?"

"Lots of reasons," he said quietly.

"Like what?" I asked. Mom and Dad always said I was a heavy sleeper, and even a wrecking ball wouldn't wake me up.

"I don't know, too much on my mind, I guess."

"Like what you want to do the next day?" I asked.

"No."

"The next book you want to read?"

"No," he sighed. "When I was younger, I used to stay up thinking about all kinds of good stuff that got me excited, like Disneyland or skateboarding, but now I just think about . . . different stuff."

"Like bad stuff?" I asked, hoping that wasn't the case.

"Yeah." He was quiet for a second. "Like my parents getting divorced."

"What?" I flipped over so I was propped on my elbows, facing him. "They're getting *divorced*?"

He didn't roll over to look at me, but kept staring up at the sky. "Yup."

"But you moved here because of your dad's job."

"Yeah, that's what I thought. That's how Mom dragged me out here to start over fresh. I left all my friends behind in Philly because she made me think everything was going to be okay on the other side of the country." He sniffed. "And it's not."

I didn't know what to say, but I couldn't lie there quietly. "Are you crying?" I whispered.

He didn't answer, but sniffed again, really hard.

"Hoot? Are you okay?"

He angrily wiped his eyes, and stared up at the clouds instead of facing me. "No, Callie, I'm not *okay*. My brothers are gone, my dad will be gone, and, as much as I love my mom, she *lied* to me."

"But—"

"My dad got an apartment in Chicago, and I'm stuck all the way out here."

I struggled to think of something, *anything* positive to say. "But your dad hasn't really been around much anyway, right? I mean, it won't be a huge change, since—"

"Won't be a huge change?" he snapped as he sat up and turned to glare at me.

I'd never seen him angry before, and it startled me. "Well—"

"Everything is changing. I don't have a family anymore, Callie." Tears were brimming in his eyes, and I felt terrible.

Why hadn't he told me any of this was happening?

"You still have a family. They're just . . . spread out."

His expression was fierce. "You don't get it, do you?" He shook his head, still glaring at me. "Imagine your mom and dad deciding that they couldn't live in the same house, or even the same state." He took a shaky breath. "Imagine that after all their arguing, your dad decided to set up his own life, almost as far away from her as he could get, and—"

"But there isn't any."

He stared at me. "Any what?"

"Arguing," I said. "I mean, at my house."

He didn't say anything for a long time, and when he did, his voice sounded deep and gruff, like it was someone else's. "That's right. Of course, your perfect family doesn't argue."

That wasn't fair!

"My family's not perfect, Hoot."

"Sure they are. It's all sunshine and rainbows."

"That's not true! I've got Kenneth the creep, a crazy grandma, and Clay, who'll be making me change his diapers until he's in high school!"

He frowned and his lips quivered. "You've got it made, Callie."

"No, I—"

"Yeah, you do. But you're so busy worrying about what you *don't* have, like a best friend who treated you like crap, that you don't even . . . you can't see the . . . Man, I can't be around you right now."

He stood up and walked away, without saying another word.

"Well," I shouted after him, "I can't be around you right now either!"

But I sure wished I could.

For the next couple of days, I didn't see any sign of Hoot. I knocked on his door twice. The first time, his mom told me that she was sorry but he didn't want any visitors. She gave my arm a squeeze and I could tell she knew something had gone wrong between us.

Had it ever!

And it was entirely my fault.

The second time, I watched her drive away, then walked over. I saw the curtains upstairs move while I was crossing the lawn, but when I got to the front door, Hoot wouldn't answer, even after I pushed the doorbell for so long I thought my finger might fall off.

After those two attempts, I gave up.

"Where's your pal?" Dad asked a few days later, while he was making a sandwich. I was staring at a stupid TV show I didn't even want to watch.

"Hoot?" I asked.

"Who else?" He shrugged. "You guys were inseparable for weeks and now he's disappeared."

"We had a fight," I sighed.

Dad put the salami, mayo, and sprouts away, then brought his sandwich into the living room. I noticed he'd used the regular mayo instead of the healthy stuff Mom was trying to make him eat. Regular white bread instead of the whole wheat, too.

He sat in the chair next to me. "A fight about what?"

I looked at him and shrugged, my shoulders feeling almost too heavy to lift. "I don't even know."

"I'm not following you, Callie."

I explained what happened, while Dad slowly chewed.

When I was finished, he said, "That poor kid. Divorce is pretty rough."

For some reason, that annoyed me. "That doesn't mean he has to take it out on *me*."

"Callie." Dad frowned. "Has Hoot been a good friend to you?"

He already knew the answer, but I said it anyway. "Yes."

"When you were feeling down about Amy, and then when you had so much fun raising money for Uncle Danny, and when you didn't make the dive team, was he there for you? A true friend, all the time, through thick and thin?"

A whole bunch of pictures of Hoot raced through my head, like flashbacks in a movie, when they're trying to show the audience how good things used to be. But I knew exactly how good they used to be, and I knew exactly what Dad was talking about.

"Yes. He's the best friend I ever had." I could feel the prickle of tears. "In my whole life."

"Well," he said, giving me a long look. "You should be there for him through thick and thin, too, shouldn't you?"

"Yes," I sniffed.

"Callie, this is Hoot's thin."

"I know, but—"

"There's no but, Callie. The best friend you've ever had in your whole life needs *you* now."

"But I *already* let him down!" I cried, wishing I'd said something different, done something different. "It's too late!"

"That's where you're wrong, kiddo," Dad said, leaning over to rest a hand on my shoulder. "It's never too late to be a true friend."

The tears were streaming down my cheeks, and my nose was running. "He's not talking to me," I confessed.

Dad took another bite of his sandwich and chewed thoughtfully before swallowing.

"Then write him a letter." He gave me a final pat on the back and sipped his regular (not diet) soda.

It wasn't a bad idea. I could write down exactly how I felt and Hoot could read it whenever he wanted to. Even if he wanted to stay mad for a while and didn't open it right away, at least he'd know I had something to say. When he was ready, the ball would be in his court.

I'd been feeling lost without Hoot and confused about how to fix things between us, but after talking to Dad, I felt like I had a plan.

A good one.

I spent the rest of the afternoon working on the letter, to be sure I got it just right. I practically sweated over parts of it, and after scribbling stuff out, crumpling up pages, and having to sharpen and resharpen my pencil about five hundred times, I was finally ready.

I invited Dad up to my room so he could read it, but when he got there and settled into the chair at my desk, I knew I couldn't sit still while he did.

"I'll read it to you," I told him, reaching for the page.

"You know, Callie, this is between you and Hoot. You don't have to share it with anyone else."

"It's okay," I told him. "I want to."

I cleared my throat in preparation. My hands were shaking. I'd never written a letter like this before, and even though I thought it had turned out really well, the truth was, I was nervous to read it.

But I knew I could trust Dad, and I wanted him to be proud of me.

"Here goes," I said, then cleared my throat again.

"What is this, a radio play or something?" Kenneth asked, poking his head in the door.

Oh, fish sticks.

"Buzz off," I told him. The last thing I needed was the world's biggest smart aleck barging in.

"Callie," Dad warned, then turned to Kenneth. "We're having a private conversation here, bud. Why don't you head downstairs?"

"Whatever," Kenneth muttered, then left us alone.

"Okay," I said, finally ready to read. "Dear Hoot, I am so sorry for not being half as understanding about your problem as you've been about *all* of mine. And I do have problems, but they seemed a lot worse before you moved in next door. You made everything better for me, and I wish I did the same thing for you. I know I can be selfish sometimes, and I'm sorry about that, too. I'll work on fixing it. I promise. You are the best friend I've ever had, in my whole entire life, and I would *never* want to wreck our friendship. I miss you a lot and I hope you can forgive me someday for being a jerk. From your very, very sorry friend, Callie Boone."

Whew.

I looked up and saw that Dad was nodding.

"Good job, Callie. You took some responsibility there, and that was a very grown-up thing to do."

"It was hard to write," I admitted.

"Some of the most important things in life are hard to do. That's part of what makes them so important."

He stood up and gave me a bear hug, the tight kind I loved, even though they made me feel like my ribs might crack. "Thanks, Dad," I mumbled into his chest.

"You're welcome. Thank you for being the daughter I'm always proud of."

"You are?" I asked, my heart catching in my throat.

"I am," he said, winking at me before leaving my room.

That felt just as good as writing the letter, and I couldn't help grinning to myself as I put it in an envelope and headed for Hoot's house.

This time, I didn't knock. I slipped the envelope underneath the door and headed back home.

I didn't see the upstairs curtain move, but I figured he'd find the letter soon enough.

Chapter Fourteen

I didn't hear from Hoot for three whole days.

He didn't stop by, call, or send smoke signals.

I tried to be patient, but couldn't help looking out the window several times a day to see if he was getting ready for a bike ride or heading out in the car with his mom.

But I didn't spot him once.

I didn't know if he'd read my letter yet, or if he even knew it existed. Suddenly, I understood why the post office offered delivery confirmation.

Before dinner one evening, I helped Mom unload groceries from the car and I was so bored, I told her I'd take Clayton to the park to keep him out of her hair while she cooked.

"Thank you, Callie," she said, rolling up her sleeves to wash and peel the carrots. "That's very nice of you."

I got Clay's wagon from the garage and he screamed with delight.

"Be back in an hour or so, okay, Cal?" Mom said as we left.

Dad was mowing the lawn, so Clay and I waved to him as we came down the driveway. The poor guy was sweating a river, thanks to the afternoon heat, so I quickly zipped back inside to get him a cold glass of water.

"Thanks, Callie," he said, taking a big gulp. "That really hits the spot."

"No problem." And it wasn't. Lately it amazed me how easy it was to make the people around me happy.

Everyone but Hoot anyway.

I missed him terribly.

Clay and I made it to the park, where there were about a million little kids swarming the swings, monkey bars, and teeter-totters, like a bunch of hyperactive ants.

I let my brother loose and made sure I watched extra carefully while he played with the others.

It was pretty boring.

I sat on a bench and sweated, wishing the park's Splash Center wasn't closed for repairs. Thinking of Dad's ice water, I wished I'd thought to bring cold drinks for us, too.

To pass the time, I daydreamed about diving, of course. I knew that if I wanted to make the team next time, I'd have to be even more committed to practice. There would be more to learn, and if I wanted to be really great, like Dad, there would be even more hard work ahead of me.

What I knew for a fact was that all of the effort would be worth it.

After forty-five minutes or so, I was so hot and uncomfortable, I couldn't stand being at the park anymore. I was glad it was time to go home.

Clay's face was red from the heat and all of his running around, so I figured he probably needed to cool down, too. After only a bit of whining, he climbed back into the wagon for the trip home.

He seemed about fifty pounds heavier than he'd been on the

way there and I knew that the second I got inside the house, I'd be much more interested in a shower than dinner.

But when I turned the corner onto our street, it didn't look like I'd be having either.

There was a police car parked right in front of our driveway, with its lights flashing.

Next to it was an ambulance.

Grandma!

I forgot how hot and tired I was and pulled Clay's wagon as fast as I could, knowing in my gut that something terrible had happened.

I remembered how awful it was when she had her stroke, and how the doctor said it almost killed her.

I could barely catch my breath as my feet pounded against the pavement.

Why did I yell at her the day Animal Control took the ferrets?

Why did I get so annoyed when she cranked up the volume on the TV?

Clay didn't know what was going on as we bumped and rattled on the sidewalk, so he started to cry, then scream. But there was no time to comfort him. I had to get home.

As soon as we reached the driveway, I lifted him out of the wagon, grabbed his hand, and half-dragged him across the front lawn.

There was lots of running around and shouting from the paramedics, but I couldn't understand most of the big words they were saying.

"What's happening?" I asked. My voice was too quiet for anyone to hear.

Clayton squeezed my hand tighter and I gave him a little squeeze back, trying to reassure him.

At least I'd remember Grandma, but Clay was too little.

I watched the paramedics close the doors of the ambulance, shaking their heads sadly, and I knew she was gone.

I clenched my fists so I wouldn't cry.

That was when I saw Mom.

She was hugging Kenneth, and her face was wet with tears. My heart stopped as I realized it wasn't just about losing my grandma. She was my poor mom's own mother. I felt a sharp jab of pain as I thought about what it would be like to never see Mom again, and had to push the idea out of my mind right away.

It hurt too much.

I pulled Clayton over to her, feeling awful for what she was going through.

When Mom looked up and saw us, her face crumpled even more. She let out a big sob and loosened her grip on Kenneth so she could pull us all into a group hug. Before I knew it, I was crying, too, and Kenneth was shaking.

I knew it was a weird thing to think at that moment, but I imagined it felt good for Grandma to look down on us from Heaven and see how much we loved her.

We stood that way for a long time, all four of us breathing hard and crying.

When I could finally talk, I said, "I'm sorry, Mom."

She pulled me even closer to her, but didn't speak.

"I'm sorry, too," a familiar voice said from behind me.

Confused, I let go of my family and turned around.

"Grandma!" I shouted, shocked and amazed. "I thought something happened to . . ." I was even more confused. "I thought maybe . . . what . . . ?"

"Oh, honey," Mom said, tears streaming down her cheeks. "It's not Grandma."

I looked from her to Grandma, but they didn't say anything more.

I turned to Kenneth, whose eyes were all red and puffy from crying.

"It's Dad," he said softly.

I covered my ears so I couldn't hear any more.

Chapter Fifteen

Callie," Mom said, pulling my wrists down to my waist.

I was crying—big, gasping sobs. My head was throbbing, it was hard to breathe, and all I could think about was the way the paramedics shook their heads.

I would never see my dad again.

I started to tremble, tears streaming down my face.

I couldn't look at Mom, Kenneth, Grandma, or anyone around us. My ears were buzzing and all I wanted was for the whole world to stand still for a minute or two, to go completely silent, like I was underwater, so I could somehow think of a way to make it all stop.

"Callie, listen to me," Mom said, gripping me tighter and forcing me to look into her eyes. "Dad had a heart attack."

That only made me cry harder.

"But, honey," Mom continued, "he's alive."

And then the whole world really did stop.

I held my breath for a second or two, afraid to believe her.

He's alive?

"He's not out of the woods yet," Grandma said.

Mom gave her an angry look before turning back to me to say,

"They've already stabilized him, right here in the driveway, and now they're taking him to the hospital."

The buzzing in my ears started to fade away.

"I want to go," I said, watching as the ambulance lights flashed. He was inside.

Alive.

"No, Cal. I need you kids to stay here with Grandma."

"Can't we—" Kenneth started.

Mom shook her head before he could say more. "I'll go with Dad and I'll let you guys know what's happening as soon as they tell me."

"But, Mom—" I whined.

"No buts," she said, wiping her eyes and walking toward the ambulance, only looking back once with a scared smile.

She climbed into the front seat and in a few seconds they were gone.

"I can't believe this is happening," Kenneth said quietly.

"Me neither," I whispered.

"Let's get out of this heat." Grandma took Clayton's hand and started walking toward the house. "I'll make some iced tea."

Iced tea?

My dad had a heart attack and I was supposed to sit around and drink iced tea?

I knew he was her son-in-law, not her son, but didn't Grandma even *care* what happened to Dad?

I watched her and Clayton walk in the front door and all I wanted to do was shout at her.

"Come on, Cal," Kenneth said, awkwardly putting an arm around me to guide me into the house.

By the time Clayton was down for a nap and the three of us

were seated at the kitchen table, I was still angry at Grandma and terrified about Dad.

"How did it happen?" I asked, staring at my full glass, ice cubes tinkling like wind chimes.

They were both silent for a moment, but I didn't make eye contact with either of them. I just sat there and waited.

"He was mowing the lawn," Kenneth finally said. "I was in my room, reading, and I didn't even notice when the motor stopped." He choked a little and I looked up to see there were tears in his eyes. He quickly wiped them away with the back of his hand. "I didn't *know*."

I felt like I was being torn in half. Part of me wanted the details and the other part was too scared to hear them.

"So, did he fall down?" I asked, deciding it was better to know than to wonder.

"He collapsed," Grandma told me, nodding. "I don't know how long he was on the ground before the dogs went crazy."

"If they hadn't barked like that, none of us would have known anything was wrong," Kenneth said.

I thought about our hyperactive wiener dogs and I couldn't believe it.

"Babs and Roger saved him?" I asked.

"No, Grandma saved him," Kenneth said, giving her a shy smile.

"What?" I asked, turning to stare at her.

She didn't say anything, but Kenneth spoke again. "She gave him an aspirin."

I was totally lost. We weren't exactly talking about a headache. "An aspirin?"

"Well, of course I shouted at your mom to call nine-one-one first," Grandma told me.

"But . . . an aspirin?" I asked again.

"I had some in my purse," she said, shrugging.

"The paramedic said it's the best thing to do when someone's having a heart attack," Kenneth told me. "He said people are more likely to survive *and* it can mean less damage is done to the body." He pointed to Grandma. "She's the hero."

I turned to stare at her again. This time, it wasn't in anger, but awe.

"What?" she asked, shrugging again, like it was nothing. "I saw it on *Oprah*."

I jumped up from my chair and gave Grandma the tightest hug ever.

"Thank you," I whispered, feeling guilty for all the times I'd rolled my eyes at her.

We didn't hear from Mom for hours, but it felt more like days. Kenneth and I kept busy playing Battleship, then Risk, kind of like the old days, before he started spending every minute in his room.

The games helped to distract us, but every now and then we'd look at each other and I'd end up crying again.

I just wanted to see Dad.

When Mom did phone, she only spoke to Grandma, even though Kenneth and I were both right there waiting to talk to her.

Did she still think I was a little kid who couldn't handle anything?

"He's going to be in there for a few days of observation and testing," Grandma told us when she hung up. She looked at each of us and took a deep breath. "You kids are old enough to know what's going on, so I'm not going to sugarcoat it. He's got two big blood clots blocking his heart and they may have to operate."

"No," I whispered, imagining some stranger cutting Dad open.

What if something went wrong on the operating table?

What if the surgery didn't work?

"Your mom says they'll know more tomorrow."

But they ran their tests and didn't know anything the next day.

Mom stopped by the house twice, but we only saw her for a few minutes each time because she was anxious to get back to the hospital. And when we did see her, she looked so tired, it made me worry about her *and* feel even more scared about Dad.

She still wouldn't let us see him.

Despite everything that was going on, and the stream of neighbors dropping by with cookies, casseroles, and sad faces, I still hadn't heard a word from Hoot.

The next morning, I woke up feeling totally normal, but that only lasted for a couple of seconds.

My stomach in a twist again, I remembered that everything had changed.

My dad had a heart attack.

My throat closed up, like I was drowning, and then the tears streamed down my cheeks. I started whispering, "No, no, no," to myself, as if I could make it all go away.

But I couldn't.

Clayton must have heard me, because he opened my door and peeked around the corner. I didn't want to see anybody right then, but I let him come inside anyway. He walked over to the edge of my bed and said, in his tiny little voice, "Ith Daddy working?"

"No," I said, shaking my head.

"Where did he go?" he asked, tilting his head to one side.

"Mom!" I called, but of course she wasn't there and it was Grandma who came to the door.

"Oh, Callie." She sat on the bed next to me and pulled me up into a hug. At first I wanted her to stop, but then I relaxed against her chest and I never wanted her to let go. I could hear her breathing and feel her pearl necklace against my cheek.

"Me too, me too," Clay begged, so we let him join us.

"It's going to be okay," Grandma whispered in my ear.

I desperately wanted to believe her.

That day, while we waited to hear from Mom, Clay kept asking everyone who stopped by our house where his daddy was. Sometimes he would act like he was playing a game of hide-and-seek and he'd wander around the house, looking in the closets and under the furniture, asking, "Daddy?"

I wanted him to be quiet, like the rest of us, but he was just a little kid and didn't know any better.

That afternoon, the doorbell rang.

"Who is it?" Grandma called from the living room.

"I don't know yet," I said, moving toward the door.

"Are we expecting company?" she asked.

"I don't think so."

"Maybe another casserole," she sighed. "We'll never be able to eat them all."

When I swung the door open, he was standing on the doorstep.

Hoot.

His hair was short, like a buzz cut.

Hoot.

"We were away, Callie," he said very quietly, and I could see the tears in his eyes. "I didn't know."

I bit my lip hard to keep from crying and nodded to let him know I understood why he hadn't come by sooner. I was just glad he was there, but now I was too emotional to say anything.

I opened the door wider and Hoot followed me inside.

"We're waiting to find out if he needs surgery," I said softly.

He nodded.

He sat next to me on the living room couch and stayed there for the rest of the afternoon. Clayton wanted to watch his *Dora the Explorer* DVD, so we sat through that, then *The Muppet Movie*, and Hoot never pushed me to say anything. It felt safe, knowing he was right there, like he was protecting me.

My silent partner.

It was the best thing he could have done. There was no pressure on me to smile or make conversation, or pretend that everything was okay. I could sit there and let my mind wander wherever it wanted to.

Where it wandered was to good memories of Dad, and I let them fill me up.

I thought about our early mornings at the pool, the secretive winks we always shared, and the way he liked to pretend he was the host of a cooking show when he barbecued.

Every now and then, I thought about the sweet or fatty treats I'd sneaked to Dad over the years and felt terrible about it, as though *I'd* somehow caused the heart attack.

A panic built up in me whenever I thought about that. It was hard to catch my breath, and my eyes stung with tears, but Hoot didn't say anything.

I pushed the thoughts to the back of my mind.

When I was ready, I confessed, "I'm really scared, Hoot."

"Me too," he said. "And I'm sorry, Callie. I'm sorry about our fight, about your dad, about everything."

"Me too," I whispered back.

He cleared his throat. "I've got something for you." He stood up and pulled a light blue box from his back pocket. It had a tiny white bow on it.

He handed it to me and I didn't want to unwrap it, certain that there was nothing on earth that could make me feel better.

"Open it," he said.

I lifted the lid and then a layer of white tissue paper.

Underneath was a very simple and plain silver bracelet.

It was pretty, but I didn't know what to make of it. "Thank you, Hoot."

"It's engraved," he said, gently taking it from me and turning it so that I could see the letters inside.

"IKYMI.AAYCB?" I asked, totally confused.

"There wasn't enough room, so my mom thought we should abbreviate it."

"Abbreviate what?"

He cleared his throat and blushed slightly. He pointed to the first letter, then each one that followed as he said, "I know you'll make it. After all, you're Callie Boone."

I jumped out of my seat before he could say another word. I wrapped my arms around him and gave him the tightest hug I could as the tears ran down my cheeks.

"Oh, thank you, Hoot," I cried. "It's perfect."

"You like it?" he whispered.

"It's the nicest gift I've ever gotten."

And it was true.

The most perfect gift in the world, from the best and truest friend I'd ever had.

Chapter Sixteen

The next day, Dad's doctor decided not to operate. When we heard the news, Grandma, Kenneth, and I jumped around the kitchen shouting with joy.

Little Clay jumped around, too, even though he had absolutely no idea what was going on. Even Uncle Danny was there to shout with us. (It turned out that his mysterious nights away from home were spent at his *own* home. He and my aunt were getting back together!)

Mom picked Kenneth and me up that afternoon to take us to the hospital. She still looked tired, but I could tell she was relieved.

So was I.

We were finally going to see Dad!

On the way there, the happiness faded a bit and I started to feel nervous instead.

"If they don't operate, what happens to the big clots?" I asked.

"Don't worry about all of that, honey," Mom said, changing lanes. *Don't worry?*

I couldn't decide if that made me feel more upset or angry.

"I can't help worrying," I told her, wishing she would see that I was old enough to handle it. "Can't you just tell me what's happening? I'm not a baby, Mom."

"Callie," Kenneth warned.

That wasn't enough to stop me. "Did you even mean what you said about wanting us to be close?"

Mom glanced at me in the mirror, then back at the road, biting her lip. "You're right, Cal. I'm sorry." She cleared her throat. "Dr. Gonzalez is going to dissolve them with a special drug. Your dad is very lucky."

Good news! I felt a smile on my face for the first time in days.

"That's the first and fast part of treating him. But it won't be over yet," Mom added.

"It won't?" Kenneth asked.

I stopped smiling.

Maybe I didn't want to know, after all.

"The doctor and I have talked a lot, and Dad is going to have to make some serious changes."

"Like what?" I asked, trying not to sound too scared.

"Well, if he wants to be healthy, and we know he does, he's going to have to work very hard on diet and exercise."

"No more buttered popcorn," Kenneth said.

"No more maple bars," I added. That seemed simple enough.

"That's right," Mom said with a smile. "We all love Dad and we've got to help him. The Boone family is a team, and we're going to win this one together."

We were a team.

When we arrived at the hospital, we rode the elevator to the ninth floor. As we walked down the hall, the soles of my shoes squeaked on the linoleum. If I was anywhere else, I would have twisted my feet to turn the squeaks into squawks, but I knew better.

We passed a nurse's desk with a huge bouquet of the prettiest flowers I'd ever seen, but even they weren't quite enough to make the hospital the kind of place I'd want to hang out in.

It smelled too weird.

"Here we go," Mom said, resting a hand on my shoulder when we reached Dad's doorway. "He's pretty tired, so he might not look quite as lively as you're used to."

I looked at Kenneth, who seemed to be as nervous as I was.

"Okay," I said, my voice sounding like I was underwater.

"Just be yourself," Mom said.

"Okay," I said again, this time a little louder.

I remembered Mom saying how small Grandma had looked in her hospital bed, but that didn't prepare me for seeing Dad.

When I turned the corner, my whole body went stiff.

He was sitting up, with his eyes closed, looking very pale. The tubes and wires hooked up to a bunch of machines next to him were like something out of a sci-fi movie.

Kenneth quietly gulped and said, "Wow."

All I wanted to do was run away.

Mom rested her hands on my shoulders again and gave them a squeeze.

"It's okay, Cal," she whispered.

The sound of her voice woke Dad up, and when he opened his eyes I realized I'd been holding my breath.

I slowly exhaled and did my best to look "normal."

Dad looked at us for only a split second before he started to grin. "Hey," he said.

I stared at him, my body quickly filling with relief.

Even with all of those tubes, and the pale yellow hospital gown, that big smile made everything seem okay.

"Come here, you guys," he said. His voice was raspy, like he hadn't talked for a long time.

Kenneth and I walked over to him, but when we got to the bed, I think we were both afraid we'd hurt him by touching him, so we just stood there, our hands hanging at our sides.

"I don't get a hug?" Dad asked, lifting his arms toward us.

Kenneth and I both leaned in and Dad gripped us in a bear hug that may not have been his usual rib-crushing tightness, but it was pretty darn close.

"I'm sorry I gave you guys such a scare," he murmured.

"Never again," I said into his shoulder, hot tears stinging my eyes.

When he let go of us, I turned to see that Mom had tears in her eyes, too.

Dad cleared his throat. "I'm sure Mom has told you that I need to get serious about my health."

"And that you need our help," I said, nodding.

"I do. Are you guys up for it?" he asked.

Kenneth and I both nodded as Dad waved Mom over to the bed and took her hand, holding it out in front of him. Kenneth added his hand to Dad's, and I placed mine on top of Kenneth's. If Clayton had been there, his sticky little hand would have been in the mix, too.

"We're in this together," Dad said.

"All for one and one for all," Mom added.

And in that moment, I felt like we would really make it.

For dinner, Grandma made her secret-recipe spaghetti and we sat at the table, trying to pretend everything was okay.

As soon as the meal was over, Mom pulled us all into a tight group hug, then left for the hospital.

I climbed the stairs and my feet seemed to weigh a thousand pounds each. In fact, my whole body felt heavy and tired.

I passed my parents' bedroom and swallowed hard when I saw a crumpled bag of potato chips on Dad's bedside table.

Breaking his habits wasn't going to be easy.

When I got to my room, I flopped on the bed and stared at the ceiling.

It was still light out, so I could barely see the glow-in-the-dark stars Dad and I had stuck up there.

We should have taken the time to lay them out like real constellations, but I'd been too impatient.

Mom would say that's the story of my life.

But how was I supposed to change that?

What could *I* do?

I thought about it for a long time, wishing I knew even the first step to take.

And that's when it hit me.

If I wanted to change anything, I couldn't just cross my fingers and hope for the best.

I needed to make *plans*.

I got up and moved to my desk, grabbing a notepad from the drawer.

Just make a list of everything that needs to be fixed.

I put pencil to paper, and by the time I was finished, it was a very long list.

Some of the things were big, like Dad's health and me not making the Seals, while others were smaller, like my messy room.

I took a deep breath, trying not to be overwhelmed, then turned to the next page. At the top, I wrote "<u>Solutions</u>" and started on my second list.

When Dad got out of the hospital, I would watch his snacking. If he wanted a treat, I'd bring him an apple or some grapes.

No more candy.

No more chips.

I knew Mom would officially be in charge of his diet, but we couldn't leave it *all* up to her. If we were going to help Dad, each of us had to do our part.

The Boones were a team.

And as soon as Dad was home, we could take walks after dinner each night.

All of us.

Together.

Even if we only started with short trips around the block, it was something. And we could build it up from there.

But that might not be enough to save him.

I closed my eyes.

We have to try.

When I opened them again, I moved to the next item.

"Didn't make the team."

When Dad was feeling better, he and I would be back in the pool again. But until he could drive, I would get there myself, which meant convincing Mom I was old enough to take the bus. There was a schedule downstairs and I was sure I could figure it out.

I would train three days a week, doing all the things Dad taught me to do.

Even laps.

No matter how much I hated them.

If he could sacrifice his treats, I could tackle the backstroke.

As I wrote my ideas down, I felt a bit better, so I kept going.

"Bedroom is a disaster area."

I would start using the laundry hamper in my closet.

I would put away toys and books as soon as I was finished with them.

Easy.

Pretty soon I was almost halfway down the list.

Well, a third of the way.

I would help Clayton with potty training.

I would be a better friend to Hoot by paying attention to what was happening in *his* life, instead of only worrying about mine.

The solutions were coming quickly, until I came to "not enough friends" and got stuck.

Oh, fish sticks.

How do I fix that?

I leaned back in my chair and tried to think.

I tapped my pencil against my forehead.

I bit my lip.

I stared at my calendar.

School starts pretty soon.

I thought about the girls other than Amy and Samantha who were in my class last year.

Jen Holland was nice, and she'd invited me to her birthday party.

Hmm.

I *could* call Jen and ask her to go school supply shopping with me. Sure, it would feel weird to go with someone other than Amy, but maybe it would be more fun.

Maybe.

But what if Jen already bought her supplies?

What if she just plain didn't want to go with me?

I thought about it for a second or two.

You keep trying.

If Jen said no, I could call Heather Pearson, who was my partner in science class and played the clarinet.

If Heather didn't work out, I would try Sonia Santiago. We'd sat at the same lunch table a few times, and she was really funny.

Hmm.

Maybe I'd call Sonia first.

And if none of those girls wanted to go with me, I'd think of someone else.

Just like taking care of Dad and making the Seals, I had to keep trying, even if I failed.

More than once.

Which was totally possible.

I kept working on the solution list, and every now and then, I'd remember a new problem and add it to the other page.

It seemed like I might never have everything sorted out.

When I started to get a cramp in my hand from all the writing, I read over the solutions.

At least I'd come up with good ideas.

Some of them might even work.

I glanced at the problem list again.

It was getting longer by the minute.

What if I only get through half of it in the next six months?

What if it takes a whole year?

It doesn't matter. Just keep trying.

I left the pages on my desk and pulled the hamper out of my closet. I started filling it with dirty socks and the T-shirts I'd left on the floor.

When I was finished, I crossed that item off my list.

One down, twenty-six thousand to go.

Don't stop.

I put away the Monopoly game I hadn't played for weeks, then straightened the books on my shelf.

I put my hands on my hips and looked at the mess, then got back to work.

And as I cleaned up the deck of cards that had spilled out of their box, I glanced at the letters engraved on my bracelet.

For the first time ever, I really understood that what Dad had been telling me all along was true.

I know I'll make it. After all, I'm Callie Boone.

Acknowledgments

As always, a big thank you to my super-agent, Sally Harding, for encouraging me to try something totally new and rolling with the results.

I'm also grateful to Jean Feiwel for taking a chance on Callie, and to both Jean and Maria Barbo for being so easy to work with.

And finally, thanks to my parents, Sally and Stuart McDonald, who helped me get my first library card, and to Beverly Cleary, who will always have a place on my bookshelf.

Thank you for reading this FEIWEL AND FRIENDS book.
The Friends who made

After All, You're Callie Boone

possible are:

Jean Feiwel, publisher

Liz Szabla, editor-in-chief

Rich Deas, creative director

Elizabeth Fithian, marketing director

Holly West, assistant to the publisher

Dave Barrett, managing editor

Nicole Liebowitz Moulaison, production manager

Jessica Tedder, associate editor

Caroline Sun, publicist

Allison Remcheck, editorial assistant

Ksenia Winnicki, publishing associate

Elizabeth Tardiff, designer

Find out more about our authors and artists and our
future publishing at
www.feiwelandfriends.com.

OUR BOOKS ARE FRIENDS FOR LIFE

31901047263985